SECRET OF THE MOUNTAIN

by

MARGARET HARDISTY

Illustrated by
SONDRA KEENA

Carodyn Publishers
Lafayette, California

OTHER BOOKS BY MARGARET HARDISTY

For Husbands and Wives:
Forever My Love; Harvest House Publishers, Eugene, Oregon
Your Husband, Your Emotional Needs; Harvest House
How To Enrich Your Marriage; Carodyn Publishers, Lafayette
California (Co-authored with George Hardisty)
Plan Your Estate; Carodyn Publishers (co-authored with
George Hardisty)

For Children Ages 4-9:
Orange Teeth and Blue Ears
*Terry Fussimo learns about eating and nutrition from
his conscience, Conn Shuns;*
Ploppidoo A Plotzer
Danny Deedle Dawdle finds working with Dad is fun!
I Want What I Want When I Want It
Beggity Peggity quits begging from her parents.

Secret of the Mountain

Copyright 1988 by Margaret Hardisty

Published by Carodyn Publishers
Lafayette, California
ISBN-0-913143-04-9

"I'M GOING TO A SPECIAL PLACE, DANNY.
IT'S FULL OF WONDERFUL SURPRISES. AND...AND I
THINK IT HAS A HUGE SECRET IN IT
SOMEWHERE. SOMEDAY I WILL TAKE YOU
THERE, I PROMISE, BUT NOT YET."

CONTENTS

In memory of Thomas and Theodora Quimby whose courage and sense of adventure laid the foundation for wonderful stories for young people who like to dream of better things for their lives.

Chapter 1

Thomas Jefferson Quimby

Bessie sat darning the tip of her long black stocking, her tongue held between her teeth and over to one side, trying with all her might to mend it so her toe wouldn't shove through again and the stitches would look neat in the bargain.

She was doing quite well at her task, which might be expected, for although she was but ten, she was more apt to be thought of as twelve or so. Perhaps that was a natural result of being an only child of a mother who firmly believed that children should be perfectly obedient and act more like grownups than boys and girls, and of a father who was fairly along in years when she was born.

For all of that, except for the fact that she was teased a great deal about her name, for people had started calling their cows Bess, she was a happy and contented girl. She was not as docile as her domestic skills might indicate. She could have some delightful giggly times and be tempted to all sorts of harmless mischief. Furthermore, she could beat almost any boy her age in shinning up a tree, paying scant attention to the fact that her skirt would slip up beyond her knees.

Unduly hot for March, it was, nevertheless, a satisfying day, for her mother was in the kitchen, humming and making cinnamon rolls. Her father had a steady job at Knudsen's Planing Mill and all was right with the world.

But while she placed stitch after careful stitch, something was happening, of which she knew nothing as yet, that would turn everything around as surely as a top spins when one gives it a whirl. For, right that very minute, Thomas Jefferson Quimby had swung into a swift stride, his long steps carrying him out of the office at the mill, and down the dirt road that wound beneath wheat colored hills.

He scarcely noticed the distance it took along South Washington Street to bring him to the business section of Sonora, a mining town that had been settled rather rapidly, years before, during the California gold rush, but which had grown to a fairly good sized metropolis that boasted five churches. He jogged over to Green Street and then marched along the wooden sidewalks past the Opera House and the hotel, barely glancing at the gray and weatherbeaten stores whose tall false fronts perched above their roofs, advertising the wares within.

He lifted his hand in greeting to a small knot of men leaning against the square pillars that framed the porch of the Union Democrat, but didn't slow his pace one bit.

A man of determination, if not always of wisdom, Thomas was liked wherever he went, for his manner was warm and friendly and a twinkle was ever present in his blue eyes. His brown mustache, which hung down as far as his chin on each side, bounced when he walked, although, rather than giving him a comical appearance, it simply served to make him look jauntily handsome. However if he were lying perfectly still, one wouldn't think of him as anything but simply nice looking.

He pulled open the door to the assay office and clomped to the counter. "Mornin,' Clem. What did you find?"

"Good day to you, Thomas," came the greeting. "Been hearin' rumors about you," he continued, looking at some ore he had in a test-tube. "They true?"

"Probably I would hope not," Thomas laughed. "What's being said?"

"That you might be leavin.'"

"I'm surprised you heard about it. I haven't told anyone my plans."

"Don't have to. You've ordered a wagon and horses and other supplies. Word gets around."

"My family doesn't know yet."

"Best you tell them, before someone else does. Your gold dust tested out good. It'll give you some travel money."

A half mile beyond the town, Thomas jumped up three steps onto the stoop of a small, clapboard house which perched happily on a hill under an enormous oak tree, and swung open the front door.

"Pack your things, Princess, we're heading for the mountains!" he laughed as he burst through.

Bessie jumped up, spilling her sewing. Her eyes sparkling, she knelt quickly to scoop it up, feeling a tingling in her stomach.

"To the mountains?" she squealed. "But don't you have to work this week?"

"Not this week or next!" he chuckled. "We're going to move! South and east of here."

Bessie sobered, her smile melting away.

"B-b-but, Daddy," she stammered, just as her mother came out of the kitchen, "we just got settled in our new little house."

"Bessie," her mother admonished, smoothing her hair with one hand and her apron with the other, "don't be disrespectful to your father," drawing out the last word so it sounded like "fahthuh."

Bessie had given up long ago trying to convince her parents to speak like westerners. Theodora Waters Quimby had come from the New England States, as had Thomas. That was where folks left r's off words and used other sounds that seemed comical to the Quimby's daughter.

Sometimes she would tease, saying, "MotheRR, can't you put your RRR's in youRRRR WoRRRds?" and her mother would retort, "We do have an English heritage, Child," which meant she had no intention of changing what she thought was proper.

In fact, she believed in being proper with regard to all areas of life, which belief she had dutifully attempted to pass on to her daughter. Bessie, however, although she tried most of the time to live up to her mother's expectations, couldn't quite get the knack of it, for all intents and purposes, and was forever forgetting this rule and that, which sometimes brought censure or punishment from her mother, or at the very least, an exasperated sigh.

Theodora Waters Quimby was by no means a frightening woman, however, for, even though she might be described as strict, which came as a matter of course for her, due to her own upbringing, she had a kind and patient manner.

An attractive, small lady, hers was a quiet, inner strength that had brought her through a number of tragedies with a determined glint in her eye which always looked forward, rather than behind.

But no one was thinking of that right then, or word pronunciation or behavior, except, perhaps, the behavior of Thomas, who was throwing his family into a bit of a shock. Theodora turned toward her daughter. "Bessie, your hair is untidy. Go to your room to comb it."

Not that her mother was encouraging vanity. It was her contention that one's looks were neither to be a matter of pride nor lamented, which suited Bessie just fine. The child was far more interested in rolling rusty barrel hoops down the street with a stick or thrashing through forests than being worried about how she looked. That is except for her hair. There were times when she would like to have had other than braids that resembled skinny strings, for her hair was so fine that, when it hung loose, a strong puff of someone's breath could set it standing all about her head.

No, the real reason she was being sent to her room was because her mother believed firmly that children should not be part of serious adult conversations. That conviction may have been influenced, at least partially, by Bessie's tendency to chatter incessantly, once permission was granted for her to voice her opinion.

Nor was she allowed to argue her case. Just recently, when she was not permitted to sit in on a discussion about the family finances, she said, "But, Mother, I AM ten!" which was considered impertinent and, as a result, she didn't get a cup of hot cocoa that night before bed.

So, having learned from experience, she obeyed immediately,

and went to her room, not wishing to detract from the matter at hand.

She left the door ajar, however, and then, to ease the guilt she felt for wanting to eavesdrop, she walked over to her "bookcase," which was a wooden apple box standing on end with three treasured volumes in it.

She picked up her comb which lay on top of the box, formulating a plan. It was her thought that, while she was combing her hair, she could walk rapidly around the room, slowing each time near the door where she just might accidentally hear snatches of her parents' conversation. Since the room was small, it would take no more than five very long steps to complete each cycle.

Her plan worked well enough, and in fact, she was able to catch glimpses of their faces as she made each pass.

"I QUIT the mill," her father said, the blue of his eyes shining more brightly than ever.

"Quit!" It exploded out of Theodora as if she'd been poked in the stomach.

"This morning," he said. "I just walked right into Mr. Tannin's office and quit!"

His wife reached for a chair to steady herself.

"Theodora, Darling," he said gently, "I can always get another job in a mill."

"But, Tom," she said quietly, "you've had a steady income in...goodness knows how long, and..."

He interrupted her eagerly, as he always did when he had an idea with which he wanted her to agree. "Wait until you hear me out." He began to pace.

"You've heard me speak of Henry and Ellen Crocker. Wonderful folks! First time I met him was in 1882, in Stockton, at the old Weber House. We hit it off from the beginning. I've seen him a few times since, here and there. Well, our paths crossed

5

again when I went to Chinese Camp last week. There he was in the livery stable. Mr. Crocker, himself! And he recognized me straight off. Theodora, he's offered me a wonderful opportunity. He wants us to stay at his place where I can work as a handyman part of the time for our board and room.

"A handyman!" Theodora whispered. "Thomas..."

"It's perfect!" he went on. "It means I'll have time to get on with my prospecting. Rich gold has been taken out of the mountains near where they live and I just have a feeling we'll find what we've been looking for. I've been thinking about it all week, and suddenly I knew what we should do."

Bessie pulled her comb through a tangle. They'd been through this before, many times. And unless her mother was able to reason with him, it looked as if they were going to pull up stakes and do what they had done so often: hope to find a bonanza.

It wasn't that he hadn't found gold in the past. He had supplemented their income many a time with panning in the clear mountain streams, and working in old abandoned mines or placer diggings that others had left behind. But he'd never found anything that came close to a fortune.

Bessie sighed. This was the first home they'd ever owned. Not that it was unusual in any way with an unpainted outside and inside walls which were covered with butcher paper to cover the cracks between the boards. But to Bessie, whose life had been a nomadic one, it was the most wonderful house in the world.

A lot of work had gone into it, too. Her mother had decorated the windows with curtains she had sewn and had braided a lovely round rug for the floor, made from many colorful rags they had collected. And what about the needlepoint cover for the little stool and the matching pillow for her mother's rocking chair that Bessie had done herself? Not that they couldn't take those things with them, but... Executing a v-e-r-y slow step by the door, she looked wistfully at the different colored threads with which she had struggled for weeks, and wondered. Would there ever be another house that would belong just to them?

Feeling a lump come into her throat, she caught a glimpse of her father, still pacing the floor, "talking a blue streak," as her mother would say. Suddenly he asked, his eyes flashing with excitement, "What do you think, Theodora?"

"Tom, I think you have a bit of gypsy in you," she answered, trying to smile.

He gave a "WHOOP!" pulled her out of the chair, and whirled her around the floor until she begged, in good humor, for mercy. Bessie responded to the fun, jumping up and down and clapping her hands, laughing and laughing, making no pretense of staying away from the door any longer.

"ADVENTURE AHEAD!" Thomas shouted, stomping happily outside to get things ready to go. Theodora turned toward her daughter with a look that said, "Settle down, now. We have things to do."

Without a word, but giggling inside of herself, Bessie started packing.

Chapter 2
Old Long Nose and Spitter

The journey was hot and dusty, with Bessie getting the worst of it, tucked in the back among their belongings as she was, but when the driver geed and hawd the horses through Jamestown and Chinese Camp, she forgot her misery, wiped her hair from her eyes and stared curiously at the residents, including several children who gawked back at her.

Later on, there was Priest's Grade to liven things up a bit. Although Bessie had heard about that part of the road from her father, she wasn't prepared for the twisting narrowness of it as it seemed to snake straight up into the sky.

"Princess!" her father shouted at her over the groaning of the wheels, "Up ahead is the grade I told you about. It's got a bunch of names: Moccasin, Rattlesnake Hill, Old Priest's Grade..."

She nodded and tried to shift her position. Her arms and legs were painfully cramped, holding onto items, trying to keep them from sailing out of the wagon when they hit rocks and bumps, so when the wagonmaster pulled off the road and cried, "Everbuddy out!" she untwisted herself and climbed down, thankful to be released from her prison.

"Yew all haf ta carry sumthin'!" the driver ordered. "It's one thousand five hunnert and seventy five feet straight up. Horses cain't be expected ta do it all."

At first Bessie started up the hill eagerly, but since she had loaded herself down heavily with some of their possessions, and the day was very hot, with no shade along the way, she soon felt as if her legs were heavy stumps, reluctant to make the next step.

"Here, Bessie girl," her father laughed, relieving her of some of her burden. "About a mile up, there's a spring. We'll stop there for rest and water."

And then, to keep her mind occupied, he said, "Walk over here, closer to the edge. See? The canyon is called Grizzly Gulch."

"There goes a jackrabbit, Daddy. Did you see it?"

"Couldn't spot him. You've got sharp eyes, Princess. Good place for him, though. That's Toyon brush down there. Keep your eyes peeled and you'll see a gold mine or two in the side of the mountain facing us."

When they came to the spring, where a large turnout enabled the driver to pull in to water the horses, she found new energy and climbed eagerly up a wooded hillside. Soon she skidded down the steepest bank on her backside to where her mother stood with a tin cup and a sandwich for her, and then skipped over to the side of the turnout where the spring had turned into a little stream that ran swift and clear, hugging the contour of a hill before it poured over the road and into the deep canyon. She would have been much happier drinking from it directly, on her knees, slurping the water up through pursed lips, but other folks had stopped at the turnout as well which, to her mother, constituted a semblance of society, thus demanding proper drinking from a cup, so Bessie dutifully acquiesced.

She was about to dip her cup in for some of the cold, crystalline water, when in trouped some Miwok Indians. Three half naked braves rode proudly to the stream where they dismounted, allowing their thirsty horses to take long drafts of water as they kneeled down and drank, wiping their faces with their bare arms when they stood up.

But what fascinated Bessie were the women. They had heavy loads on their backs held in place by decorative leather straps bound to their foreheads. One girl, who looked about 13, was carrying a small child in her pack, along with blankets and other items. She bent far forward in order to keep her balance. Another had deer meat piled high in skins. Flies were buzzing around the meat and lighting all over the woman.

The squaws sat down with much grunting and groaning. Bessie worried about how they were going to get a drink unless they took the packs off, which, it was soon apparent, they had no intentions of doing. The men ignored their ladies, so almost before Bessie realized what she was doing, she filled her cup with water and, walking very carefully so it wouldn't slosh out, took it to the eldest of the women and offered it to her.

The old woman cackled something Indian to the others, her delight showing in her speech as well as her eyes which were almost lost in the many wrinkles that puckered up her face. All at once the squaws began to jabber to each other, laughing and saying things to Bessie, which she couldn't understand. Then the venerable lady took the cup, drank the water, and handed it back. Her benefactress ran to the stream again, dipped out another cupful and offered this one to the woman with the deer meat on her back. One by one she served them, enjoying herself as thoroughly as they.

The girl with the child on her back didn't say anything when it was her turn, but, after giving the tyke a drink, she watched Bessie with her deep dark eyes while she satisfied her own thirst. One of the other women said something to her, motioning to their young sympathizer, but the girl shook her head so nothing more was said, which left Bessie wondering.

When it was time to go, the women tried to get up but couldn't. Congenially, the braves pulled them to their feet, leaped onto their horses, carrying their bows and arrows, and rode out onto the road, leaving the squaws to trail behind on foot.

The girl with the papoose looked up as she walked by, still bent nearly double with the weight she was carrying. Bessie grinned and said, "Goodbye." The girl didn't answer, but her eyes softened and a slight smile came to her lips.

Bessie turned her attention to the stream again, planning to get a drink for herself, but her mother appeared, took the cup and handed her another. "You must never drink after another person, Bessie, and especially strangers," she admonished.

No sooner had the Indians left than an old prospector, with scraggly hair and a bushy white beard, stopped on his way downhill. He looked at the Quimbys carefully, squinting. He smiled then, showing that several teeth were missing.

"Jist wanted ta' be shure you folks wasn't robbers."

He took off his ragged heavy pack and laughed. "Not thet I have anythin' robbers ud want ta steal. Course, there's muh hide, but they wouldn't want that neither. Too tough." He cackled at his own joke, sat down, leaned against a bank, and went sound asleep. Bessie watched, fascinated, as his mouth dropped open and his snores began: BZZZZ... SNAW... SNORT... pwwwwsssssss.

Before long, his symphony was drowned out by the heavy stomping of horses' hoofs, as two men rode into the turnout. The one who appeared to be the leader had a long nose and small eyes set too close together. That, with an obvious cruel twist of his mouth reminded Bessie of a wolverine she'd seen once. Old Long Nose, as she dubbed him, dismounted with a string of curse words aimed at his partner who wasn't moving fast enough to suit him.

The partner was chewing tobacco and spitting it every few seconds so that when he got off his horse, he turned his head and a brown blob landed right on the boot of Old Long Nose who let a screech out of him and ordered the spitter to clean it off.

They were raising such a ruckus that Bessie's father spoke to their driver about moving on, but the driver was fixing a wheel on the wagon and it wasn't finished yet. Nor did he want help in doing it, so they just had to wait.

The spit difficulty was solved without incident, but soon after, Long Nose noticed the prospector who was asleep. He took out a rope and, laughing, started toward the old man with a grinning Spitter following along behind.

Bessie ran over to her father and tugged on his shirt. "Daddy, those men! They're..." But she didn't need to finish.

Her father reach into the wagon and pulled out a pry bar. In a few long strides, he stepped in front of the old prospector, facing Long Nose and Spitter.

"You fellas want something?" he asked.

"Move aside," Long Nose snarled. "We ain't got no quarrel with you."

"Matter of fact, you do, if you're planning on bothering my friend here," Thomas said solemnly.

"Friend?" Spitter interjected. "He ain't got no friends. He's just an old sourdough. We was jist gonna' fun 'im."

"I reckon as how you aren't going to fun anybody. Now, mount your horses and move on."

Long Nose laughed. "Who's talkin'? There's two of us -- one of you."

"Two of you makes half of me," Thomas said, taking a step toward them, slapping his hand with the bar. "Get movin'!"

Old Long Nose moved his hand toward his holster. Bessie gasped, goose pimples popping out on her arms. Just then, the wagon driver and another fellow who had stepped off a carriage, walked over to stand beside her father, facing the troublemakers, too.

Old Long Nose stopped grinning and said to Bessie's father, "I never forgit a face, Mister. We'll meet agin, only next time the odds are goin' ta' be on my side." Then he and Spitter mounted and rode off.

Chapter 3
A Bit of Society

Soon after the incident with Long Nose and Spitter, the Quimbys were on their way again, the horses puffing up to the top of the grade and lumbering straight to Priest's Station. Since the station had become famous among travelers, Bessie was thrilled to hear they were stopping there for the night, her first time to sleep in a hotel.

The highlight, in her estimation, was having dinner in the dining room that evening, for she had never eaten in a public place and the thought of it being one of such reputation was awesome. To heighten the excitement, Mrs. Priest, who owned the establishment with her husband, stopped by their table. She was so lovely that Bessie fixed a fascinated gaze on her, taking in every detail of her face, her hair and her dress; that is, until her mother nudged her under the white tablecloth with her foot.

When Thomas told Mrs. Priest that they were going to be living at Henry Crocker's place on Big Oak Flat Road, she brightened like the flickering lamps that hung on the walls.

"Then we'll be meeting again!" she smiled. "Mrs. Crocker and

I are very good friends. They come down here often, and you must, also. You shall stay as our guests." Bessie's mother's eyes shone at that, for, even though she had lived very humbly since she married, she longed for the nicer things in life, and because Thomas was gone so often, she became lonely for adult company, especially with those who were well bred.

Much to Bessie's surprise, Mrs. Priest, who was aware of the child's adulation, turned to her. "And you, my dear, are welcome anytime," she smiled graciously.

One glance had told her that the girl had never known luxury, but she had been taught good manners, of which Mrs. Priest definitely approved. Had Bessie realized that the lady was also thinking that she was an extremely pretty child, with no notice at all of her unruly, baby fine hair, she would have dismissed it as flattery, rather than sincerity. Certainly no one had ever indicated to her that she was anything other than what she thought about herself. And in her opinion, she was definitely homely. Her parents had never told her otherwise, although it must be noted here that they were fully aware of their daughter's fine features and winning ways. Not wishing to spoil her, however, they kept their opinion to themselves.

Their hostess then moved to another table, so gracefully, as her mother called it, that Bessie decided right then and there that she would try to copy her as soon as she was alone. Before they ate, her family bowed their heads and said a prayer of thanks without speaking out loud, but when Bessie looked up, she saw several people staring at them, some looking quite amused.

"Never mind, Princess," her father said quietly. "What they think doesn't matter."

She sat very tall after that, acting as if she were grown up herself, taking extra care not to spill her soup or drop food in her lap. But she almost ruined it all by gulping quite loudly upon seeing a girl across the room, older than herself, kicking her feet back and forth like some little kid. She slouched, too.

Bessie tried not to stare, but the girl was all dressed up in a red velvet dress with a beautiful white cape draped across the back of her chair. Not that she was envious. She'd never had an expensive dress, but she couldn't ever remember wanting one, either. They couldn't afford it, and besides, where would she wear it if they could?

Nor did she feel even a twinge of jealousy over the girl's long, thick, curled hair, for even though she might wish for her own to be different, Bessie had never known what it was to be covetous.

She did bite her tongue instead of her potatoes and gravy, though, when she heard the girl say loudly, 'No! I won't!' to her mother, who was trying to get her to eat her carrots. Her father urged her to eat her cabbage then, and she raised a bigger fuss.

The girl's father begged, 'Please, Leslie,' but his daughter stuck her tongue out at him. To his credit, he did become upset at that, so he stood up, took her hand, and said, "Let's go see the pretty sitting room." He walked out, pulling her along. The mother called after them softly, "Keep in mind she's very tired, Nathaniel."

"It's about time they did something," Bessie thought as they passed the Quimby table. She made the mistake of looking at Leslie just at that moment, and the two girls' eyes met. The other made a face at her, which took her by such surprise that she knocked her glass over, which, fortunately, was empty except for a few drops of water. Nevertheless, her mother looked at her sternly, and she felt disgraced, embarrassed to glance around the dining room another time.

She looked down at her plate, and then gingerly took a bite of cooked carrots, which were not her favorite. But food was food, her mother always said, and they were blessed to have it. Her father often stated that it was an insult to God to refuse to eat what He sends someone's way.

Bessie wasn't at all certain that God sent cooked carrots to anyone but she was painfully aware of the fact that, if she had acted like Leslie, no matter how tired she was, she would have been taken out of the room and lectured, or maybe even spanked. Then she probably would have had to write, "I will NEVER speak to my parents disrespectfully again," over and over.

She felt terribly sorry for Leslie's father and mother, who looked distraught. People all over the dining room were frowning at them. But she supposed it was their fault, letting their daughter get away with that sort of conduct. After all, they were bigger than she.

She squeezed her eyes shut for a second to make a quick silent vow to herself. "When I grow up," she whispered in her mind, "and if I ever am a mother someday, I will NEVER, EVER let my children talk back to me and act like Leslie."

But growing up and being a mother was a bit weighty for a young girl who, by the time dessert was served, was too tired and sleepy to eat it, so she was given permission to leave. Once in their room, she stumbled to the cot she'd been given, which was placed next to her parents' bed, and snuggled down between the cold sheets, thankful for the heavy patchwork quilt which pressed heavily on her.

She whispered a few prayers, trying to keep alert enough to finish each petition to the Heavenly Father. The prospector they'd seen at the spring that day came to mind, but before she could ask that he be blessed, the clearness of the picture faded and Leslie floated in, yelling at the Indian girl while Old Long Nose and Spitter were shooting their guns at Thomas' feet.

If Bessie had known that there would come a time when, except for the prospector, she'd meet each of them again under some very unpleasant circumstances, she might not have drifted off to sleep as peacefully as she did. As it was, she knew nothing until a bird, twittering dawn, crept onto the windowsill to awaken her.

Chapter 4

Crocker Station HO!

A Rufus Sided Towhee hopped within six feet of Bessie as she sat on a tree stump waiting. He cocked his head, sizing her up with one shining red eye. She longed to hold him, stroke his brick red breast and then watch him spread his white speckled, dark gray wings as he flew from her hand. But even as she contemplated it, she rejected the thought. Wild things were their most beautiful when left alone.

She had managed to stay decorous all morning, which pleased and surprised her mother no end. She pulled her knees up and rested her chin on her arms. The driver unloaded all their belongings from his wagon and rumbled off to drive back to Sonora. Her father had arranged for everything to be stored in the hotel shed, so it could be brought to them later in the week.

As for them, they were going to ride on the Yosemite! They climbed aboard the elegant stage, her father offering a strong arm because the step was nearly as high as Bessie's waist. She sat down on the velvet covered seat, delighted, and looked out the window to see if there was someone to whom she could wave goodbye. That was when she saw them. Over by the livery stable, leaning against the wall, was Old Long Nose and Spitter, the same men who had threatened her father on Priest's Grade. They were looking right at their stage. A little chill went through her and she pressed closer to Thomas.

He saw them, too, because he said, "Don't worry, Princess. They're just a couple of bullies who've jumped a few claims up in these parts."

"Except for the incident on Priest's Grade, I didn't realize you knew them," Theodora commented solemnly.

He shook his head. "I don't. I just know of them. Jake Gasten is the long-nose fellow. His dull witted partner is called Maxie. The law has tried to catch the two of them in one of their law-less acts, but they've never been able to. We have no reason to be afraid. We don't have a claim they can jump, and nothing much they could steal. You can tell by looking at them that they haven't been very successful at whatever they do."

Trying to appear as if she weren't, Bessie looked at the two men out of the corner of her eye. Claim jumpers were people who stole a gold claim from someone. That she knew. She decided to forget about them, but down inside, she was worried, wondering if they would meet them again someday.

The driver rattled the reins, yelling, "HO!!", drove them onto Big Oak Flat Road and headed up into some of the most beautiful country they'd ever seen. They rumbled along behind four sleek horses that pranced down the road as if they were happy to be out.

Great rows of big trees lined their way: Ponderosa Pine, tall and straight, with their yellowish bark that looked as if someone had scrubbed them clean with a brush; Tamarack, which had bright green needles that looked like lace; Redwoods that were so tall Bessie could scarcely see the tops and some so big around that not even two big men could put their arms around their trunks and Blue Spruce which looked soft and fluffy, but which were stickly to touch. They saw one HUGE Sequoia, too, which was so immense that a stage could have ridden through the middle of it, if someone had cut a hole there.

The driver yelled down to them, "Thar's a hull stand of them big uns north an' east uh here. Worth a trip."

The forest was the home of deer, bear, cougar, raccoon and all sorts of wild creatures, Bessie knew. Well, they'd have to move over, she said to herself, for the Quimbys would soon be sharing it. She smiled, and then, even though the stage was jiggly, she fell asleep against her father's shoulder.

A few hours later, her mother's hand on her knee awakened her. "Bessie, look, we're arriving at Crocker Station."

The driver had left the main road and was guiding the horses into a clearing and toward a number of white buildings. The largest one, although not tall, like Priest's Hotel, was impressive looking with its white boards and wide porch. As they drew nearer, she could see the words CROCKER HOTEL & STATION painted in neat letters on the front wall near the door.

Suddenly Bessie had an entire mouthful of questions crying to be answered, but since she knew she would be expected to wait and see, she opened her eyes wide to see how much she could discover for herself.

The first person they saw, other than some old miners sitting out on the porch, was a youth of thirteen, who walked out of the hotel with gangling steps. By the time they pulled up, he was waiting, grinning shyly.

"You must be Mr. Quimby," he said, offering his hand. "I'm Dan Fields. I'll take your bags in for you." Thomas shook hands with him, and then introduced his wife and daughter.

Dan didn't bother to look at Bessie which irritated and pleased her at the same time. On the one hand, she didn't like being ignored by anyone, even though, with adults, she was expected not to speak until spoken to. On the other hand, boys were hardly to be tolerated with their teasing, hair pulling, showing off tendencies. So she lifted a determined chin and looked anywhere she could but at him.

As soon as they stepped into the hotel lobby, a pretty smiling woman walked toward them rapidly, with her hands outstretched. Bessie liked her immediately, for her smile was genuine and her heart warm. It was Mrs. Crocker herself.

"Mr. and Mrs. Quimby, how wonderful that you made the trip safely. And this must be little Bessie." She bustled them up some stairs, down a hall, and through one of the doors there.

"These will be your rooms for the time being. We'll move you into a cabin later. My husband is in Groveland for a few days, Mr. Quimby, so, while you are waiting for him, you and your family can explore a bit. Please feel right at home."

The main room was much larger than they expected and as soon as she was gone, they oh'd and ah'd at what they saw. It had a big brass bed, and was furnished in elegant brown wallpaper with yellow and tan borders on it.

"Oh, look!" Bessie exclaimed. She had gone into what was to be her room. Small but comfortable, it was decorated with wallpaper graced with lavender flowers. Never had she seen anything so breathtaking. "I've decided," she gasped, "lavender is my favorite color," which brought a chuckle from both of her parents.

In her room was a shelf for putting things on, and, much to her delight, she discovered that she had her own coal oil lamp. Suddenly she squealed. "A pitcher and bowl -- just for me! I'll be able to wash my face before anybody even sees me in the morning." Further exploration set her chattering excitedly, "Ohhhh, brass hooks for my clothes," which was perfectly adequate, since she had only two outfits which she wore interchangeably, "and look, Mother, there's a chamber pot under the bed that's just my size! I won't have to go outside during the night."

"Bessie!" her mother admonished, for chamber pots were not something one discussed, although she nodded with approval just the same, because they were handy when one was very ill. And certainly it would be most unacceptable to traipse downstairs in one's nightclothes to use the facilities that the hotel offered in case one did need to get up in the night.

The subject was closed, so Bessie continued to revel in her new room. Suddenly she stood very still, and then looked furtively over her shoulder. Her parents were chatting amicably and paying little attention to her. That was good, for on a small nightstand, for her very own use, was an ornate little hand mirror. Of course, her mother always wanted her to be tidy, which would be especially important while they were living in a hotel where people saw you all the time, but should she show too much interest in the mirror, Theodora might put it away for fear Bessie would begin looking at herself too much. But she

needn't have feared, for as I told you, even though others looked at her as an extremely fair child, she was convinced she was
anything but attractive, and believed that nothing would change
that fact. Thus she seldom had an inclination to look in a mirror.
But this one was so crinkly and gold around the edges, she
made up her mind right then and there NEVER EVER to leave
her room in the morning without making sure her hair and face
were, at least, neat and clean.

She touched the mirror gently and then turned to inspect the
bed and the flowered coverlet that made it fit for a princess!

Celia, the Crockers' daughter, who soon would be eighteen, as
Bessie found out later, and their son Johnny, who was two years
younger than his sister, were at the dinner they all shared together in a special corner of the dining room so they might
become acquainted. Dan Fields was there, as well, for he worked
for the Crockers and lived at the hotel. After Celia told Bessie
that Dan's dad had been killed by outlaws and his mother had
died, soon after, of diphtheria, she decided she would consent to
tolerating him, and even, perhaps, behave kindly toward him.

Celia, who was inclined toward having fun, was very friendly,
but Bessie felt shy and awkward. Her hands seemed AWFULLY
big when she spooned something onto her plate. And for the
first time in her life, she was self-conscious about the fact that
her dress was very plain, and patched, which she hoped they
wouldn't notice. She could feel her ears sticking far out from her
head, too, and was sure that everyone was laughing at her inside
of themselves.

Then she remembered something her mother had told her.
"Bessie, always sit up straight," she had said. "Hold your head
up high, look people directly in the eyes when you talk with
them, smile, and you'll fit in fine, wherever you are. Remember
this: most people are more interested in themselves than they
are in you." She tried to follow that advice throughout the meal,
although being a child of little social experience, she carried it
off rather poorly.

There hadn't been a chance for her to have friends much,
since her family had never stayed in one place very long. Nor
had she ever been to school so, during the next few weeks,

Bessie began to enjoy knowing Celia and Johnny Crocker and Dan, and although she felt like a country bumpkin for a long time, it was a new experience that gave her a warm feeling deep inside.

Although it wasn't necessary for their room and board, Theodora began to help Mrs. Crocker with washing, cleaning the

lodging houses and serving meals to guests. So, it seemed only natural for Bessie to do it, too.

"Tell you what," Celia smiled, "you can set out the silverware and napkins for now."

"Oh, please let me serve when the guests are seated, Celia. I'll be ever so careful!" Bessie pleaded, but Celia shook her head.

"There will be plenty of time for that. We'll see how well you do on the other things first."

Bessie was very careful to line the forks and napkins up perfectly, and listen closely to what she was told, so one day, Celia smiled.

"Tonight you may set the china on. Watch your step so you don't stumble. We don't want broken dishes."

And since she didn't break anything, and seemed to be satis-

factorily steady, she was privileged, one evening, to take in bowls of mashed potatoes to set before guests. It worked fine except for the time she got her thumb in the gravy and then licked it off. Celia was the only one who saw her, though, and when she shook her head very slightly, Bessie took extreme care not to let it happen again.

It didn't take her long to find out that Crocker Station was famous for its meals, and wanted to keep its reputation. Depending on the provision of the day, they would serve huge roasts, racks of venison, lamp chops, platters of fresh trout, chicken and other meats. They also served vegetables that were in season. And the pies - peach, apple,  gooseberry, mincemeat, cherry and squash - were enough to tempt even a girl who ordinarily didn't care for desserts.

"Since when did you start liking pies, Bessie?" her mother asked one evening after they had gone to their quarters.

"As soon as I was the one who wasn't making them!" her daughter laughed.

Celia Crocker was very proud of the Station. While they were all walking the grounds one day, she explained, "My mother and father first moved to this area when they married, and then, in 1880, because there was a need for a stopping place for travelers, they built this. Father named it Crocker's Sierra Resort in the beginning, but people just ended up calling it Crocker Station."

Bessie found out a lot of other things about Crocker Station. It was considered the showplace of Big Oak Flat Road. Besides miners and other travelers stopping by, people, including the famous, would come from San Francisco and other places to vacation in the summer, driving up in their carriages or wagons, their fine horses stepping high. Sometimes they were on their way to Yosemite Valley, where nature put on one of her finest and most breathtaking displays of mountains, rocks and waterfalls.

"High flutin' folks," Thomas would say, which meant they put on airs and thought they were better than others because they had a lot of money. But Bessie didn't think that was true of all of them. Some were extremely nice and treated her like she was someone special, too.

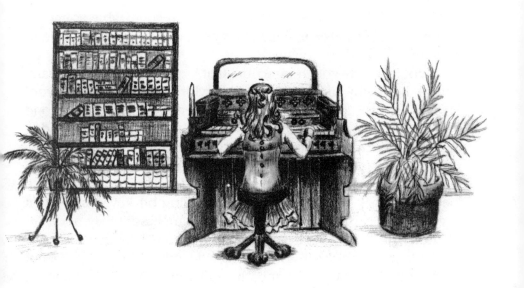

Chapter 5
The Elusive Door

Bessie looked first to the left and then to the right, and then breathed a sigh of relief. There was no one in sight. Slowly she pulled the big door open and slipped into a fairly large room that was presided over by a stuffed elk's head which hung over a fireplace. A rectangular shaped table set at one end, with chairs around it, and books and magazines on top.

But none of these were of interest to her. She walked straight over to a pump organ that graced one corner. Her secret ambition was to play it in one of the church services that were held there on Sundays, but she wouldn't tell anyone, she decided, until she could make it sound beautiful.

She adjusted the round stool, positioning it higher by swirling it around with her hand and then sat before the instrument, nonplussed. Finally, she pulled some round stops and placed her feet on the carpet covered pedals, stretching her legs out full length. She managed to push down on one pedal and press a key with her finger, so that a sound of sorts popped out, startling her.

But, even though she finally got both feet pushing the pedals and all fingers pressing the keys, nothing recognizable sounded, and not being a musical child, she wasn't quite sure what to do to change it around.

"I could teach you how to do that," a semi-deep voice said. It took her so by surprise that Bessie whirled around on the stool so fast it just kept going. She hit her knee on the second revolution, and would have fallen off if a strong hand hadn't steadied her. She looked up into Dan Field's friendly eyes.

Her face red, she stammered, "I...I'd appreciate that, Danny, but you might find that kind of hard. I don't hear the difference between music notes very well. I even sing off key. It's just that I wanted to do something special in church someday and..."

She trailed off, embarrassed. He nodded. "This guy I know... he isn't musical either. But he can do other things lots better than I can. Bet you could, too," he added eagerly. "Tell you what. It takes a long time to learn to play. Maybe it would be best if you helped me pass out song sheets, and put the chairs up before the service."

"Oh, may I?" she responded enthusiastically and was full of chatter about it that evening to her parents.

Although Mr. Crocker usually brought the message, the following Sunday a traveling preacher came through, so he was asked to fill the pulpit.

Bessie felt immensely important as she passed out the song sheets, although she was fully aware that her mother would caution, "Pride goeth before a fall, child," so she tried very hard to be humble.

After she had finished she sat in the front row, but soon regretted it when the minister began to wave his arms and shout.

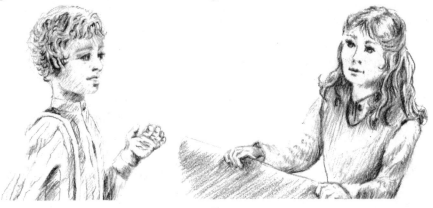

She bit her lip and looked hard at the floor to keep from giggling, for her parents would consider even a snicker inexcusable. Besides, Danny and Johnny were where they could see her, and since she didn't want them thinking that she was a silly baby, she gained control of herself by concentrating very hard on the preacher's message.

He yelled about how people sell themselves to the devil by sinning, which was just about all the time. That put them in the devil's prison, he said. Bessie shuddered at that, so was glad when he went on to say that Jesus paid ransom to the devil for them when He died on the Cross, by trading His life for theirs.

By doing that, he insisted, Jesus had unlocked the door of the prison so folks could walk out, if they wished. If they didn't walk out and follow after Jesus, they wouldn't get to go to heaven.

After talking further for what seemed forever to Bessie, suddenly he pointed right at the congregation, moving his long, bony finger from one side of the room to the other, and hollering, "Walk out...through that prison door! Walk OUT...through that prison door! WALK OUT...THROUGH THAT PRISON DOOR!"

Three times. Just like that. Then he stalked to the back of the room, into the lobby, out the front door of the hotel, got on his horse and galloped off!

Theodora, who always had enjoyed the theatre and indeed, liked to recite publicly, seemed intrigued. Thomas was smiling, amused. Danny was looking down at the floor. But Bessie was puzzling over what the preacher had said.

Naturally she knew who the devil was. God's enemy. And he tempted people to do bad things so they'd go to hell instead of heaven. But the devil's prison stumped her. She was sure the preacher didn't mean the devil's prison was one with four walls. It was a pretend place, probably, and yet..it was real. She wasn't sure she understood that.

She had felt uncomfortable when the minister talked about doing things one shouldn't, too. She wasn't REAL bad, she told herself, but sometimes she thought mean things about someone when they weren't nice to her. Or she would want to take the biggest piece of meat on the platter. She didn't think about God much, either. And there was no escaping the fact that sometimes she felt a sadness deep down inside when she thought of heaven. Naturally, that didn't make the least bit of sense, she allowed. Heaven was supposed to be the happiest place ever.

"I suppose that means I'm in the devil's prison, all right, like lots of others," she murmured and then looked down, hoping no one had heard her.

"But," she wondered, "if I did start thinking about God and wanted the sadness to go away, where would I find the prison door that Jesus unlocked? And how would I walk through it if I did find it?" She might ask the preacher about that if he came through again, she decided.

But as the days passed, there was enough to occupy her so Bessie put her questions for the preacher into a special corner in her mind where they wouldn't get in the way, at least for the time being.

March was behaving in characteristic fashion by now with nippy breezes and plenty of rain, so there weren't many guests at Crocker's as yet. Thus, except for wood that was needed for heating and cooking, and an occasional fence to be fixed, there wasn't much work to be done.

Mr. Crocker would say to Thomas, "Quimby, get on up in the mountains and prospect for gold. There's plenty there to be had, if you can find it."

That pleased her father, but Bessie didn't like it much. He came home terribly discouraged at times. The big discovery he hoped to make just never materialized. Of course, he'd always find a little gold, or a temporary job, which supplied the family's basic needs. Then, while he was below having it assayed and sold, he'd hear of a job in this mine or that, and would be gone for long periods of time.

Once Bessie peeked at her mother's diary and saw written there, "Oh, Tom, I miss you so much." Then, feeling guilty, she closed it quickly, sat in the corner of her tiny bedroom and let the tears flow, not only for her mother's loneliness but her own. She, too, missed her father, more than he would ever know.

Chapter 6
Bear!

Bessie went exploring a lot on her own as the weather grew warmer. She counted 15 cabins and other buildings at the station, including a store for the Chinese people who worked for the Crockers and the little house into which the Quimbys moved. They fanned out from the hotel on each side and behind, where they were tucked among big trees. All of the buildings perched at the top of a large meadow which sloped down to a small orchard of fruit trees, backed up by a picket fence and more forest.

At the bottom of the meadow was a little gully, in which Bessie had found a two-stamp mill. She had studied the mill, a piece of machinery that had two heavy weights which were designed to crush rock so gold could be taken out of it. She had seen larger ones, so she had shrugged and went on.

Each time she went adventuring, she'd push the perimeters a little further. One day she half ran, half walked down to Big Oak

Flat Road, determined to follow it for a distance. One man on horseback galloped by, but other than that, she saw no one. Rush Creek, which gurgled around the east end of the Crockers' property and then bubbled its way through the forest and down into the canyons, sang to her as she paused to throw some sticks into one of the deep pools that had been formed by big granite rocks which had tumbled down from a spot high in the mountains, at some time in history.

When she came to a fork in the road, she paused, trying to decide which way to go. Big Oak Flat Road, she knew, climbed steadily into the high mountains. Hodgdons' station was there, about two miles up, and the Miwok Indians somewhere beyond that. Hazel Green, a little settlement, was up there someplace, too.

"Not today," she decided and turned toward the road that swung left. She had heard a great deal about it, and was curious. Tioga Road was newer than Big Oak Flat Road, and perhaps that was what interested her. Whatever it was, she hadn't gone far when she heard BURBLE, BLOP, BLIPPETY BLOOP. She laughed! A little pool lay to the right of the road, formed by water drop-

ping off the hillside. She left the road, climbed the bank and, once on the top, which was more level, she followed the water to its source, a beautiful, wonderful little brook that flowed from a spring high in the mountain which rose above her.

She leaned against a Ponderosa Pine and looked up. "A mysterious, exciting mountain," she breathed. It was as if it were calling her to explore its gullies and canyons, probe the depths of its waters, and find delights that it had kept hidden from others.

"I HAVE A SECRET," it seemed to echo down to her.

"Well," she said solemnly, "I will find your secret, big mountain. You wait and see."

She continued her climb, following the brook, delighting in its beauty. Sometimes it was only a foot wide; other times, maybe six feet across. Mostly it was shallow, but there were pools as deep as three feet at intervals.

"Maybe I'll learn to fish really well this summer," she said aloud. Her father had cut a willow pole for her, attached a string to it and tied a hook at the end. "I might even put the squiggly worms on the hook without help."

A lovely grassy spot, covering a little bluff that hung over one of the pools, met her around a bend. Suddenly, overcome with a deep sense of well-being, she whirled around and around, looking up at the sky and laughing. This was her mountain! She'd found it herself! And she made up her mind right then and there that she would NEVER EVER tell anyone about it. Well, almost never ever. For here she would discover special places, she knew, and have surprising adventures that, eventually, would need sharing, but only at the proper time with the proper people.

She started her climb again but soon stopped abruptly, not moving a muscle. For there in the forest, across the brook and not more than 25 feet away, was a lovely Whitetail deer. The girl and the doe watched each other, both questioning.

On the deer's neck was a light tan spot in the shape of a cross. Bessie sat down on the ground slowly, keeping her eyes on her. The deer looked at her a little longer and then, not worried at all, began to graze. Finally, she bounded off. Only then did Bessie go on. After awhile, she stopped, and looked downhill. The road was no longer visible, and the trees quite thick.

It was as she was standing there that she heard a sound that startled her, because she didn't recognize it. She held very still and listened. After a bit, she heard it again.

It wasn't a bear, that was certain, she told herself. Bears were all through these woods, and Mr. Crocker had even killed a grizzly once. But generally they were shy, the Crockers told her.

"Oh, yes, Bessie," Mrs. Crocker had assured her, "If a bear hears you coming, he will go the opposite direction."

It was true, she thought. In all her ten years in the mountains, she had never seen a bear, although signs of them were in berry patches, and her father had pointed out territorial scratches they had made on trees.

She listened again, so hard she could hear her own heart beating. There it was! Up the mountain someplace. It sounded

almost like a baby. "Maybe it's a porcupine," she murmured. "Porcupines sound like babies. On the other hand," she said, her mind racing, "lots of wild baby animals have special little sounds. Even baby bears. Maybe...maybe it is a bear, after all," she whispered. "If it's a baby bear, the mother might

smell me." Since she had been taught from the time she could toddle that mother bears are very dangerous if they have a baby, and can run much faster than a child and can climb trees, she didn't stop to think any longer. She raced down the mountain, scrambling over logs, tearing at the branches that grabbed her hair, ignoring the bushes that scratched her legs through her black stockings above her boots.

For the first time in her life, Bessie was terrified. At one point, she pulled herself to the top of a large fallen tree which would give her a clear path above the brush, over which she might run. At that moment, as she looked over her shoulder, half expecting to see an angry mother bear pursuing her, she slipped. Branches and brush clutched at her as she crashed to the forest floor between two logs. Her foot jammed between twisted branches and she was wrestled into a sitting position, ending with one leg up in the air and the other held fast.

In a panic, she tried to pull her foot loose, but it wedged in tighter! A scream formed in her throat, and then a voice echoed through her fear, out of her subconscious. It was her father's warning. "Bessie, if ever you are lost or hurt in the mountains, force yourself to calm down and think things through." She stopped thrashing, and instantly was cognizant of the fact that there hadn't been a bear at all. If there had been, she would have heard a lot of crashing, besides her own.

She took a long, quivering breath, and at that moment, to her amazement, two brown hands appeared, pulled some heavy branches aside, and her foot was free!

She looked up, her heart beating wildly. Her mouth flew open, for, standing over her was the Indian girl she had met on Priest's Grade a month before, the girl who had been carrying the small child.

Bessie blinked her eyes, relief flooding through her, trying to comprehend. Had the Indians really walked THIS far to get home? The girl didn't have a papoose on her back today. She wore a soft deerskin dress, and she looked very pretty, Bessie thought.

She was terribly embarrassed as she rose to her feet stammering, "Thank you," several times, and made a silent promise to herself right then and there, "I will NEVER EVER let myself panic like that again."

Whether or not the Indian girl knew she'd been foolish, there was no way of knowing. Her face was very still. But Bessie noticed her eyes. Worry swam deep and troubled in their black depths.

Before she thought about the fact that she couldn't speak Miwok and the girl couldn't speak English, she asked, "Is something wrong?"

The Indian girl seemed to get the gist of it for she pointed at Bessie. Then she pointed to her eyes. After that she put out her hand and held it flat about two feet from the ground. A question was in her eyes.

Bessie shook her head. "I don't understand."

The girl pointed again. Then she circled her eyes with her fingers. Bessie murmured, "Have I seen something?"

This time the older girl made a rocking with her arms as if she were holding a baby in them.

"Have I seen a baby?" Bessie asked. "A little child?" She shook her head and tried to move her hands to explain, "No, I haven't seen anyone."

The girl nodded and headed downhill. Bessie, limping, started to follow, a thought nagging at her. The noise she had heard. Could it have been...? It had sounded like a baby -- or a child.

Suddenly she began to yell, "Indian girl -- wait! Wait!" but she was already out of sight, so Bessie hobbled as fast as she could, yelling as she went. When she came to Tioga road, she was relieved to see that the other girl had turned around and was coming back toward her.

"Come on!" Bessie yelled beckoning with her arm and clambering up the bank again. She cut through the brush and crashed through the trees, going as fast as she could, trying to ignore the pain in her ankle. Already having caught up with her, the Indian girl was directly behind, moving quietly and surely, hope flickering in her eyes.

Bessie led her companion to where she had been when she first heard the noise and halted, putting her finger to her lips as they listened. "I thought I heard a sound like a child up here before," she said, forgetting that her words would not be understood, "but I wasn't sure and I got frightened."

The older girl looked at her for a second and then started walking around, calling out softly in Indian words Bessie had never heard before. Then she'd stop and listen.

They moved slowly upstream, pausing every now and then, listening and calling, hearing only the scolding of squirrels and the chattering of jays.

"Wait!" Bessie cried, "I think I just..." She moved away from the stream, held her breath and stood very still. The sound came again, faint but definite.

"Did you hear it?" she asked excitedly, turning. The Indian's eyes narrowed and she called, cupping trembling hands around her lips. She motioned for Bessie to look in one direction while she moved in the other.

Bessie had walked nearly seventy five feet away from the stream, searching under bushes and logs when all of a sudden she jumped back, an "Oh!" exploding from her. Right in front of her was the sound she had heard and behind the sound was a tiny little boy, wedged between two good sized rocks, his leg cut and bleeding. His round face was dirty, and she could see where his tears had trickled down his cheeks.

"He's here! He's here!" she cried out, over and over, until the Indian girl came on the run. As soon as he saw her, the tot set up a howl. Both of the girls pushed hard on one of the rocks but couldn't move it. Then the older of the two, more experienced in the woods, looked around until she found a large sturdy stick. She placed it under the edge of the rock, and both girls pushed down on it, putting all their strength into it.

The rock moved an inch, but now they had another problem. If one of them let go of their lever to help the little fellow, the rock would roll back and perhaps crush him.

With both of them still pushing down, the older girl thought for a moment and then gave a sharp command. The little boy stopped crying, grabbed hold of a tiny fir tree next to him and pulled. The girl barked another order. He pulled harder, his breath coming in little pants.

Suddenly, he was free!

Before Bessie thought, she fell to her knees, picking him up in her arms, cooing and rocking and talking to him.

"Poor baby. It's all right. I'm sorry I didn't come sooner. Poor little boy."

The Indian girl knelt beside her, smiling, gently examining his leg. It was broken, Bessie was sure, because it looked crooked.

"Mr. Crocker can fix it." she said. "He's set lots of broken bones. And he can send for a doctor."

The Indian girl lifted the little fellow gently and they started slowly down the mountain.

When they came to the road, instead of moving downhill, she turned up, and Bessie turned with her, determined not to leave her at this point. About half a mile further, they came to two older squaws, sitting on the side of the road. They had a horse with a cart behind him which sloped down until the back part of it lay on the ground.

The women began to jabber as they came in sight, wobbling down to meet them. The girl handed the little boy to one of them who took him to the cart and laid him on some blankets. Then they began to fuss over him.

It was getting late and Bessie had been gone far too long. She started down the road, still limping, but feeling strong, joy welling up in her throat. At the bend she slowed, turned and looked back. The Indian girl was watching her. She raised her arm. Bessie raised hers, too. It seemed as if their eyes were close together, despite the distance, looking deeply into each other's soul, and as she felt that, despite her young years, she also had a distinct feeling that the time would come when she was going to need her friend's help again, and that help would be there. She turned and sped on her way.

When she arrived at Crocker's, she paused outside the kitchen door, and took a deep breath, trying to smooth her hair. She spit on her hands in an attempt to rub some of the dirt off her face, but all it managed to do was to make her look worse. In fact, Danny walked up just then and laughed. "You look like you've been prospecting. Are you hurt?" he added, looking at her foot.

"Uhhh...I'm okay," she hedged, "We can talk later. I have to help mother." He turned with a nod and she walked inside. Her mother, making pie dough, said without looking at her, "Bessie, run out to the chicken house to see if one of the hens might still be laying. We need two eggs."

She limped outside again, relieved that she hadn't been asked where she had been. The mountain with it's brook was a secret she wanted to keep. Now that a life had been saved there, it was even more precious. The Indian girl wouldn't tell. She wouldn't either.

Chapter 7
Wonderful, Delightful Home!

From then on, Bessie stole away to her special mountain as often as she could. Once, Dan tried to swing into step beside her on Big Oak Flat Road, but she said, "I'm going to a special place, Danny. It's full of wonderful surprises. And...and I think it has a huge secret in it somewhere. Someday I will take you there, I promise, but not yet."

The lad, who had no one his age with whom he could enjoy leisure time, was disappointed. He had come to look forward to his times with Bessie, for she had brought sunshine and laughter and yes, adventure and daring into his life. But he also knew the need one had for private times, so he was instantly agreeable. As soon as he had crossed back over Rush Creek, however, he turned to watch her skip along on her way, wondering what wonderful secrets and surprises were hers.

The doe with the cross on her neck appeared quite frequently, unafraid of the girl with the gentle spirit. "We are friends, you know," Bessie whispered to her from time to time, blowing the message to her on the wings of a kiss.

She didn't happen upon her Indian friend again, though, until she came to the meadow at Crocker's with a group of Indian women who had been given blanket permission by Mr. Crocker to pick the herbs that grew there. Bessie ran down to join her once, and the two girls were soon laughing and giggling as the older one showed her how to choose the rare plants.

Bessie slipped the ones she found in the finely made basket which hung down her friend's back from a deerskin thong that was bound to her forehead.

"Did you weave this beautiful basket yourself?" she asked, and then laughed at herself for she had forgotten that her words could not be understood.

Nevertheless, a few days later, Celia said, "Close your eyes, Bessie, and hold out your hands." She did as she was told, for she delighted in games. "There, now, look!"

"The basket!" she cried.

"The Indian girl sent it to you as a gift. Lucky you. The Miwoks are superb basket weavers. This will even hold water, you know."

A surprise snowfall came late in April, worrying the fruit trees which were showing off their spring blossoms and filling the air with heart thumping scents. But in three days it was gone.

Thomas, after coming back from a temporary job below, had tackled some major tasks for Mr. Crocker, but there was ample time for prospecting.

One evening he walked into the hotel with a dancing twinkle in his eye. Theodora and he couldn't talk because she was helping Mrs. Crocker serve dinner to some hunters that night, but they kept looking at each other across the room. Bessie knew something was up. She crossed her fingers, afraid they might be moving again, the last thing she wanted to do now.

Her parents skipped the group singing that evening and disappeared into the church meeting room. She was aching to go after them, but knew that would be frowned upon.

She had two huge question marks in her eyes when her mother appeared and called her to go to bed, but nothing was said except, "Your father is speaking with Mr. Crocker. You and I will have our prayer without him."

She hummed while Bessie undressed, though, and settled herself to write several letters. Her daughter lay awake for a long time, trying to figure it out. It had to be something good, she surmised, because when her mother had said prayers, she had whispered, "Thank you, merciful God, for the provision you have made for us."

Actually, it was Celia who slipped and told Bessie, the next day. They were walking through the meadow to see what flowers they could gather for the dining tables, when she said, "I'm going to miss you, Bessie."

Bessie was so startled, she stumbled. So they WERE going to move. Celia looked at her then and put her hand over her mouth, her eyes widening.

"Oh, oh. Haven't your parents told you yet?"

Bessie shook her head, chagrined. It didn't seem right that Celia knew and she didn't. She walked on, trying not to let her see the tears that were stinging her eyelids, and decided right then and there that when she grew up, she'd ALWAYS tell her children about something important before others found out. And she would NEVER EVER move all the time. She was feeling so sorry for herself that she almost didn't hear what Celia said next.

"Of course, you'll only be twenty minutes away. It'll be love-ly up there, and I'll come to visit often. You can still wait on tables with me and there'll be lots of other things I'll need help with from time to time."

"Twenty minutes away?" Bessie squeaked, blinking back the tears.

Although it relieved her mind to know that they would be close and it wouldn't be like moving, actually, she was still indignant that her parents hadn't told her first, so her voice was wobbly. Suddenly, afraid she would burst into tears and disgrace herself altogether, she began to run.

Celia soon caught up with her. They slowed to a walk, and she waited for awhile before she spoke again.

"I wasn't supposed to know about it either, Bessie. I overheard your father telling my father. He told him because he had to be sure the land was available. It is, you know."

"Wh -- What land?"

"A place where there used to be a cabin. The people couldn't find gold, so they left. So you can move without any problem at all. I think your father wanted to be sure it was okay before he told you, so you wouldn't be disappointed if it didn't work out."

Suddenly it dawned on her. Of COURSE her parents wanted to be sure before they let her know. And they HADN'T told Celia. She had eavesdropped!

All at once everything seemed bright again, even though dark gray clouds were traveling overhead and a warning mist was falling. Tears were stinging her eyes as before, but this time it was because she was happy.

"Where is it?" she asked, her voice breathless.

"Well," Celia explained as she broke off some fir boughs, "you cross Rush Creek, and turn up Tioga Road. Just a little distance farther, there's a black oak that leans and has a scarred blaze on it that looks kind of like a tear drop. That's over to the left side of the road."

Bessie looked at her, an excitement swelling up inside. The leaning black oak? Why that was almost across from her beautiful brook that tumbled down from the mountain above it.

Celia went on. "You turn right just before you get to it, follow a little stream up the mountain, and you come to a flat place."

Bessie's mouth hung open. She couldn't speak. Her mountain! Her brook! The mother deer! The Indians! This was nothing but joy! She pressed her fists tightly against her face, wanting to shout and yell and scream, she was so thrilled. But she didn't want Celia to think she was a silly child, either, so she choked out, "Please excuse me, Celia," and ran downhill as fast as she could go, her arms going round and round like a windmill, with Celia's laughter floating after her.

When she stepped inside the hotel, she smiled at everybody but said nothing. She'd had a secret before. Now she had two, and they were all mixed up together! Moving to their very own place on the most beautiful spot in the world was something she didn't want to share with anyone just then, except the people she loved the most, her mother and father.

She didn't have to look far for them. In fact, they almost ran into each other as they came out of Mr. Crocker's office.

"Princess! We were looking for you earlier!" her father exclaimed. "Your mother and I have something important we want to share with you."

Theodora chuckled. "Actually it's your father's surprise. We've packed a picnic lunch and are going off on a little tramp to see it."

"It seems Bessie has already been on an excursion," her father laughed, pointing to her feet. She looked down, horrified. Her shoes were caked with mud!

"Celia and I were picking for the tables," she said, talking too fast. "I'm sorry. I'll clean them."

But Mother smiled, "No need. We'll get our wraps and go straight off."

When they hiked down Big Oak Flat Road, crossed Rush Creek, and then turned left on Tioga Road, Bessie pressed her lips together tightly so she wouldn't be tempted to say something and ruin their surprise. When they came to the leaning black oak on the left, Thomas left the road and walked straight up the mountain to the right. Little piles of snow lay here and there among the pine and redwood needles, and the forest smelled clean and fresh.

They climbed over logs, walked on top of some, plowed through bushes and ducked through thick branches. Bessie could hear the water in the beautiful little brook which was over to the right a hundred feet or more.

They marched right up to a clearing where some old, weathered boards lay scattered about. Not because of the hike, but because she was dealing with a rainbow of emotions that were a tremendous lot to handle, Bessie's heart beat so hard she thought it would explode.

Thomas grinned and turned to his wife, "Well, Theodora, what do you think of it?"

She said nothing but walked around the clearing, explored the surrounding areas and found the brook. Then she crossed her arms and said with a smirk, "Thomas Jefferson Quimby, you are something special."

He laughed. "Do you like it?"

"I love it," she said, putting her arms around his neck and kissing him.

None of the discoveries Bessie had made on her mountain was more surprising than seeing her mother hug and kiss her father! Her mother was not one to show her affection in front of anyone! She whirled around to face her daughter.

"Bessie, would you like to live here?"

"L-live here?" the child whispered. "Actually live here?"

"It's going to be our future home, Princess," Daddy announced. "And I promise you both, we'll never leave it."

"One should never make promises, Thomas," Theodora sounded a warning. "Only God knows the future."

But Bessie couldn't hold it back any longer. She cried out, "I LOVE it! I LOVE YOU!" Then, with a shout, she began to zig zag around trees, crashing through bushes and jumping over logs. "Bessie," she heard her mother calling, "be careful! You're going to hurt yourself!"

Bessie laughed delightedly at her mother's declaration that she was going to hurt herself, for she seldom did, except for a few scratches or a tear in her dress. And what did that matter? This was HER mountain. She stopped running for a moment and, out of breath, stood looking up at its towering heights. She had discovered several of its secrets, including the fact that this was where they were going to live. But somehow she felt that the biggest secret of all was still known only to the mountain. Well, she would discover it someday, too.

In the meantime, these were HER woods. This was her playground. Here is where she had spent hours by herself, breathing the fresh air, making friends with the chipmunks, chewing on pine gum. She was HOME!!

Chapter 8
Tripsy

There was a flurry of activity after that. Theodora insisted that their cabin be properly planned, so there were several walks to their mountain to measure ground and transfer dreams to paper.

One such day dawned so gaspingly beautiful that they set out early. By noon the sun was still alone in the sky, with no threat of clouds, and the air warm enough that the unanimous decision was to relax a bit after they ate.

Bessie knew right where they should eat their lunch. It was beautifully green, the brush soft and lacy and the trees so perfectly shaped, that it seemed to her almost as if Heaven had come down to earth there.

Theodora had cut big chunks of bread she'd baked the day before, put slabs of thick butter on it and filled the slices with roast beef and onion. She had also baked an apple pie.

A jug of coffee was in the box, too, but Bessie wasn't allowed to drink it. She didn't care, because she had tried coffee once, sipping some from her father's tin cup, and spit it out. "I'm sorry, but that tastes awful!" she had declared, which drew her parents' laughter.

There just wasn't a drink in the whole world as good as the water in the brook which bubbled along, just a few feet away, Bessie thought. Cold. Delicious. And pure as a new snowfall.

Theodora had a book she'd brought along to read, *Female Piety - The Young Woman's Friend* by John Angell James. She had purchased it as a gift and wished to be certain it was as fine a volume as she had been led to believe before presenting it. As Bessie looked over her mother's shoulder, Theodora wrote inside the front cover:

> For
> Celia M. Crocker.
> From,
> Mr. & Mrs. Quimby
> on her 18th. birthday.
>
> Blessed are they that do his Commandments, that they may have right to the tree of life, and may enter in through the gates into the city. Rev 21 - 14,

The words brought the preacher back into Bessie's thoughts when he shouted that day in church, "Walk out...through that prison door!" According to the verse her mother had written, you had to live right to go to heaven. But the preacher had said you had to walk out of the devil's prison to get there. Well, maybe they worked together somehow, but there still was the puzzle

---

Note to reader: This is the actual note written by Theodora Quimby, 100 years ago.

of where the door was and how you got on the other side of it.

To make it worse, her mother complicated her thinking by saying, "Listen, Bessie," and then proceeding to read from the book she was giving Celia:

"Lay the basis of all your excellences in true religion -- the religion of the heart -- the religion of penitence, faith in Christ, love to God, a holy and heavenly mind. No character can be well-constructed, safe, complete, beautiful, or useful, without this."

After that she read silently, as if she had forgotten her daughter were there, so Bessie slipped over to the brook to build a little mountain road in the sand, still puzzled. Maybe she would need a holy and heavenly mind, like the book said, before she could find the prison door that opened to freedom and life forever. She sighed. That seemed like a nearly impossible task. But perhaps she ought to try it.

Not knowing quite how to go about doing it, she decided it might help to press the palms of her hands together, pointing her fingers toward heaven and walk around with her eyes rolled upward. But she stumbled several times and her mother said, rather sharply, "For goodness sake, Bessie, whatever you're doing, quit!"

Then she remembered what Danny had said one day. "Nobody lives a perfect life, Bessie." That was true, she had to agree. So, there must be some other way to find the door besides trying to look holy and heavenly minded, and attempting to act perfect.

When Thomas awakened from a short nap, he grinned and said, "Let's go exploring, Princess. Want to join us, Mother?"

"Thank you, but I'm enjoying myself immensely," she answered, not looking up from her book.

Everyone knew Thomas' real intentions. Exploring to him meant prospecting, for once a man has a dream, and any determination at all, he will continue to overturn every rock of experience to fulfill that dream. Nor was it without basis. The old timers declared that there was more gold in the Sierras that never had been found, than had. Not that getting rich was what Thomas was after, really. He'd often quote the Biblical injunction, "The love of money is the root of all evil."

"Well, maybe so," Bessie thought, "but it would be nice if he'd find enough gold so I didn't have to wear patches on my dresses when I went to town, or served dinner at Crocker's."

Thomas had gone some twenty yards ahead of his daughter when she heard him call softly.

"Bessie. Up here. Easy now."

She tiptoed ever so carefully to where he was, and there, under a bush, lying very quietly, not moving a muscle or blinking an eye, was a very small, spotted fawn.

"Don't touch him," her father said in a low voice, but he needn't have said anything. Bessie knew not to touch a wild baby animal, because that would leave a human scent and its parents might abandon it. It seemed to her very sad that animals were that much afraid of people.

"You adorable little fellow," Bessie whispered, for she had squatted down to watch him.

Thomas moved away, walking as quietly as an Indian through the trees and through the underbrush. When he returned, Bessie knew immediately from the look on his face that something was wrong. "What is it, Daddy?"

"Princess..." he hesitated, and then, looking carefully at his daughter who had grown tall and strong in the pureness of the mountain air, he decided she had to face the tragedies of life as well as the joys. He led her to a spot in some tall brush. She stared, a sick feeling moving into her stomach, for there, on the ground, was the mother deer. She had been shot.

All of a sudden Bessie gasped, "Daddy, I...I know this deer. See the c-c-cross on her neck? She and I have sort of been friends!" And she burst out crying.

She was still alive, so Thomas hiked back to Crocker's to get something to pour in her wound. Nothing he did could help her, though. She was too far gone, and she died later.

"It makes me furious when a hunter doesn't keep looking until he's found an animal he's shot," Thomas growled. "The poor thing suffered for...who knows how long? Trying to get back to her baby. Besides, what was he doing shooting a doe anyway?"

As they walked sadly back to the fawn, Bessie swiped at her tear stained face with her sleeve, vowing silently to herself, "I will NEVER EVER shoot a deer. AND, if someone else shoots one, I will NEVER EVER eat any of the meat if it's a mother deer they shot, unless I'm starving or something. And I NEVER EVER will speak to anyone again who shoots any deer unless they really needed it for food...unless, maybe, it's my daddy."

As they reached the fawn, she crackled a branch loudly by accidentally stepping on it, but he didn't move. That's when Bessie gasped for the second time.

"Daddy, look!" she whispered, pointing. "The cross. It's on the baby, too!"

"Well, what do you know about that!" he exclaimed. He lifted the frightened little animal up gently in his arms.

"We'll take care of him, Bessie. He'll be your little pet."

Bessie was quite certain that her father and Mr. Crocker went back for the dead doe later because the Crockers served fresh venison for dinner that night. She started to ask as they and their friends all sat at the long rectangular table, but her mother fixed a steely gray stare on her that said, "You keep quiet."

She also was expected to eat an adequate helping of everything that was on the table, without the slightest look of a complaint, so when the venison was passed to her, she pretended it was beef steak.

As she thought about it, though, beef wasn't a whole lot different than venison. After all, she liked cows, too. But then she reasoned, as she struggled to get her pretending apparatus working, beef always came from a steer, which was a father bull that had been fixed so he couldn't be a father. Since bulls frightened her, she didn't mind so much eating one of them.

Still struggling with her emotions, she looked down the table at Danny who, understanding her turmoil, made a ghastly face at the meat, which made Bessie giggle. That brought a disapproving look from her mother. But after that, the unwelcome portion on her plate went down fairly easily.

Raising a fawn was a challenging task, Bessie discovered, but it was fun, too. For one thing, it was discovered that HE was a SHE. Then Mr. Crocker let Danny and her make a little pen for the little deer right beside the kitchen. At night, they put her in the adjoining woodshed so a cougar or coyote couldn't get her.

Danny had promised to show Bessie how to teach the fawn to drink milk, so the day after they brought her to Crocker's,

he instructed, "You did warm the milk like I told you, didn't you?"

"Of course," she said indignantly.

"Okay. Now, put it there on the ground under her nose. Put two of your fingers in her mouth, like this, see?"

Bessie squealed when the little fawn grabbed hold of her fingers and sucked vigorously.

"Now, move your hand slow like, down toward the bucket -- that's it -- and into the milk. See? She's drinking by herself."

"It worked! It worked, Danny. You know, you're mighty smart!"

He looked embarrassed but pleased, and after that, he taught her a number of things, like how to take ticks off the little animal.

"I know. You use turpentine," she said. "That's what Daddy has to get them off my head when I have a tick."

"There's an easier way. Let's see...ah, here's a tick. Watch. You get a good grip on it with your fingers, and then twist counterclockwise, like this. See? It came right out, and it didn't even bother the fawn. It's still alive, too."

"Ugh!" she answered, but found a tick on her pet herself and twisted it right out.

The little deer became a favorite of everyone at Crocker's, but Bessie was the one she followed around like a puppy dog. Danny acted a little left out at times like that, so Bessie encouraged him to spend time with the fawn, too, and when he did, she didn't bother them.

In a few weeks, they let her out during the day, but she always stayed close to Bessie, Danny or the back door, and at night, she'd go right to the woodshed.

One day they were watching her cavort in the meadow, and Dan asked, "How come you haven't named her yet?"

"Well, I've been thinking about it," Bessie ventured. "See how she trips all the time? Do you think it would be silly to call her...Tripsy?"

She waited anxiously for his reaction, which was several moments in coming, for Danny had proved to be a good friend whose opinion had begun to matter to her.

"Guess it's as good of a name as any," he finally nodded. "Sounds like something a girl would think up. I gotta' get to my chores. See you."

Bessie hugged herself. Danny liked the name. That meant he thought she had good ideas. Suddenly she was running and calling, "Tripsy! Come on, girl. Tripsy!"

The men soon started building the cabin, using some old lumber Mr. Crocker had on his place, and before long, a little house nestled among the big trees on Bessie's special mountain.

The women, including Bessie, for children were expected to do their share, scrubbed the floors and walls, put up wallpaper, hung curtains they had sewn and placed dishes in the cupboards which they had cleaned with stiff brushes.

After that, the stoves were moved in, the stove pipes run through the holes in the roof that had been cut, and the furniture was added.

When the stool and rocking chair pillow were put in their place, one could hardly fault Bessie for looking at them covertly and admiring the needlepoint she had done. For one thing, they were a reminder to her of that day in Sonora when she hadn't wanted to move. Like a little old woman, she clucked her tongue and shook her head as she muttered, "My, how the time has flown!"

She quickly found her youth again, however, hugged herself and felt terribly glad that her father had made the decision to search for his fortune again.

The rest of the heavy work in the cabin was done by Thomas alone. Among other things, he built a pen for Tripsy by the door to the woodshed which was attached to the end of the house, and could be entered from the kitchen or directly from the outside. They would be able to bring her in if there was any danger.

Although some children might associate a woodshed with unpleasant memories of just punishment, Bessie, who was past the spanking age, loved it. She helped her father stack cord after cord of fresh cut wood for the stoves, breathing deeply, loving the scent.

The outhouse was put there, too, and Theodora hung a pretty curtain around it for privacy, suspending it from Lodgepole Pine logs. Although it was not a proper subject for discussion, any more than the chamber pot had been when they first came to Crocker's, Bessie had a penchant for being unabashedly outspoken.

"It's not an outhouse anymore," she declared to her mother one day. "It's an inhouse!"

Chapter 9

"I Can't Believe It!"

The night before the Quimbys moved into their house was one of mixed feelings. On the one hand, they were eager to form their own life, free of the confining boundaries set by others. Still, the time spent living at Crocker Station had been as valuable as the most coveted of treasures. Life lasting friendships had been built. Unforgettable memories had come out of adventures they felt they wouldn't trade for all the gold in the world.

Certainly the feeling was mutual. The Crockers had a surprise party for them that final evening. The various employees of the Station came with their families, as well as some of the nearest neighbors. The hotel guests were let in on the secret, as well, so when Thomas, Theodora and Bessie came into the lobby for relaxation after dinner, a great shout went up and their reaction of delight was all the Crockers could have hoped for.

At first there was the usual gathering into groups for discussions and exchange of thoughts, but after a bit, Henry Crocker urged everyone to get involved in a game of checkers, pinochle, whist or cribbage. Bessie won two games of cribbage in a row from Danny who tilted back in his chair and looked at her admiringly. "You know, for a little girl, you play pretty well."

"I play good cribbage, period," she returned indignantly. "You don't need to think you're so grown up. You're only three years older than I, you know."

"Four."

"Three. I'm ten. And even Celia says I'm very mature for my age."

He laughed at her and said, "But I'm turning 14 in a month, Miss Smarty. Come on, everyone's gathering around the piano for a sing."

"Where's the lady who usually plays?"

"She went below. Her sister is ill."

"We'd better be quiet," she whispered. "Mrs. Crocker is trying to say something."

"...but we'll manage," they heard her finish as they drew near. "We'll simply have to sing acappella. Now..." She stopped midsentence, whirled around and stared. Theodora had sat down on the piano bench and was running her fingers over the keys.

With a quizzical smile on her lips she began to play some songs. Mrs. Crocker stood there with her mouth open and Celia whispered, "I can't believe it. I just can't believe it!"

But if they were surprised then, they would be more so, for suddenly Theodora announced, "With your permission, I'm going to play a number by Johann Sebastian Bach, followed by a selection by one of my favorite composers: Wolfgang Amadeus Mozart."

Bessie, in awe, drew close to watch her mother's fingers, amazed that there was no music from which she was reading. She had known that her mother played the piano before she married her father, but she had no idea it was anything like this!

There was a lot of clapping and comments after she finished, and a man from San Francisco said, "Brava! Brava!" which was something people yelled in operas and concerts when they wanted to do more than clap for a woman who performed, but Bessie thought it sounded a bit silly.

Theodora, fully aware of the fact that she was creating a small sensation, suddenly nodded at Thomas, played some chords, and their audience received another surprise as he began to sing. Not

that Bessie hadn't heard him before. He'd always sung bits and pieces of songs as they traveled or when he worked outside, but she had never heard anything as beautiful as this!

Once again, the small gathering clapped enthusiastically, and asked for more, but Thomas said, "Thank you, but we have exhausted our musical repertoire for this evening. It has been well over ten years since we have had the pleasure of performing, and we are a bit rusty. However, my wife will be happy to accompany all of us in a group sing."

There was an admiring rustle as those listening responded to that. Many songs later, Mr. Crocker stepped in. "Refreshments, everyone! Help yourself."

Immediately he and his wife cornered the Quimbys, but Bessie slipped away to think about the wonder of it all, planning the questions she would ask her parents when they were alone. As she was sipping a cup of hot cocoa and sucking on a piece of molasses taffy, Danny slipped up beside her. "Your mother and father are really professional! Why didn't you tell me they could do that?"

She wasn't quite sure what professional meant, but she didn't intend to admit that so she bluffed, "If the word had gotten around, the lady who usually played might have felt she wasn't wanted anymore and that would have hurt her feelings. My parents would never let that happen."

As it was, her guess was correct, but, as Mrs. Crocker said later, "Our usual accompanist will be gone for the summer, so you needn't worry a moment, and we can enjoy your wonderful music frequently, if you'll oblige us."

Chapter 10
The Locomobile

June sparkled into place like a sunbeam on the crest of a wave. The lightness and airiness Bessie felt was indescribable. She was continually running and jumping and twirling.

"You've got to come up to our cabin early tomorrow morning, Danny," she said after school one day. "I want to show you something that will knock the eyes right out of your head."

He ran all the way, for he had to fit the adventure around the chores he was expected to do before school began. But he was amply rewarded, for on their way north, robins and orioles had swooped down in red and yellow droves around the Quimby homestead to eat pyracantha berries and find other snacks.

"See, didn't I tell you?" Bessie whispered, delighted. He, just as impressed, stayed as long as he dared and then, with a tap on her arm, leaped his way down the mountain and home.

Thomas had come back from being away again, bringing some dress material to Theodora and a ribbon for Bessie. He was able to find work in a mine close by, so Theodora took the school children on frequent "tramps," up to see him.

On one particular day, as they returned, Celia met them. "It looks as if the tourists we were expecting will be coming today. Mother wonders if you would mind helping, Mrs. Quimby? And, Bessie, there are children. If you'd give me a hand in keeping them happy, I would appreciate it."

Theodora and Bessie hurried to the cabin to eat lunch. Then Theodora slipped into her new dress she had made while Bessie tackled the dishes that were in the big washpan which set in the sink.

Never having had toys, she had learned long ago to amuse herself with whatever was at hand. Washing dishes was a favorite pastime, for she could pretend that the knives were fathers; the forks, mothers; the spoons were the children and the plates and bowls were the rooms in their house.

She was just getting into some good conversations between her pretend families, speaking in a low growly voice for the fathers, and a high squeaky one for the children, when her mother called, "Hurry, Bessie. Stop dawdling!"

She quit pretending then, finished the washing, poured the sudsy water out the kitchen door onto the ground, and then moved the big pan with the clean dishes in it into the sink.

Using some potholders, she hurriedly lifted the teakettle from the stove, intending to pour the scalding hot water over the dishes.

For no apparent reason, she stumbled and the teakettle clattered to the floor, spouting hot water in all directions. She gasped, and Theodora came racing out of the bedroom. "Bessie! What's wrong?" she asked and
then, seeing that her daughter was all right, she admonished, "Haste makes waste. You could have burned yourself badly. Well, we'll rinse them with cold for now. We mustn't be late." She added, laughing, "I'll help you get ready so you won't look like an orphan," and she tapped her on the end of her nose with her finger.

As they picked their way through the stand of trees which stood between Big Oak Flat Road and Crocker Station, they saw a number of people walking around.

But rather than going through the kitchen door, Theodora said, "Come with me, Bessie. There's something you'll want to see," and she led the way around the outside of the hotel to the front where Bessie stopped and simply stared. For right there, in front of the hotel, was something she had never seen before. Her mother, who had gone on ahead, turned, smiling.

"Bessie, come quickly!"

"What is that thing, Mother?" she asked breathlessly as she ran up beside her.

"It's a horseless carriage! I read about them in the newspaper from Stockton, but...my, my, my, would you look at that!"

"A horse...what?

"A horseless carriage. A locomobile. See? Here are the seats. And this is what they steer it with. Uh, uh. Don't touch it. What a wonder! It goes along the highway without horses pulling it."

"How can it do that?"

"It has its own power," she said, inspecting it closely. "Well, we'd best get inside. Perhaps we'll get to see it work before the owners leave."

Once they were in the hotel, Bessie looked out the window at the locomobile, hoping she would see it move. It was there that Celia found her.

"Oh, there you are, young lady," she laughed. "We've got a whole load of children here, and I need HELP!"

Bessie turned with a smile. Celia needed her, and that was a compliment. Work first. Pleasure later.

As they neared the big fireplace in the lobby which was filled with blazing logs, for it was still a bit chilly, Bessie stopped dead still and stared, astonished for the second time that day. In front of her was THE GIRL! The one she had seen at Priest's Station in March. The one who had made all the fuss in the dining room. The one who had been so RUDE to her parents.

Chapter 11
Leslie

Celia wouldn't have punched Bessie in the back, except for the fact that she was just standing there gawking. But that brought her to her social senses and the introductions began.

"Bessie, I'd like to have you meet some new friends. This is Leslie..."

A warning light went on in her head, and suddenly she wished she could say she had a headache and go home. But since headaches were as foreign to her as expensive dresses, such as the kind Leslie was wearing, she was stuck with an unpleasant duty, for she had promised to help and promises were not to be taken lightly.

"...and this is her brother, Tad, and sister, Jan," Celia was saying. "Next we have Walter, from Stockton, and..." but Bessie didn't hear the rest. Leslie was looking at her with scorn and Bessie had all she could do trying to avoid looking back.

She managed to get through the next few hours but, as she told Dan later, "Leslie kept staring at me like I was a slimy slug." He laughed but Bessie went on. "She tried to take over from the very beginning by bragging about the horseless carriage, too. 'It's ours, you know,' she said to me, 'and hardly anyone has a loco-mobile. We do because my father is very successful and very wealthy.'

"Not only is she a braggart, Danny, but Leslie's a KNOW--it--all, and no matter what Celia told her, she would say, 'I don't believe that,' or 'You don't know what you're talking about.'

"Celia began to talk through her teeth, and squint her eyes, which meant she was getting very aggravated, so I whispered to her, 'It doesn't matter what she thinks. Don't pay any attention to her.' From then on, she tried to ignore Miss Prissy from San Francisco."

"So everything was okay from then on?" Danny asked, still chuckling.

"No! Nobody can ignore Leslie. She won't let you. She would walk ahead of us and stop dead still so that Celia would nearly trip over her. Then she would laugh. When Celia told us all to do something, like run and try to catch a ball, Leslie would sit down and refuse to move. If we were playing a game where we were to stand still, Leslie would run. Her brother and sister copied her, too. Honestly, Danny, I've never seen anything like her! But please don't tell my mother I said all of this. She would say I was gossiping and being unkind, and that's not allowed. Okay?"

"Don't worry. It won't go any further. Come on, I want to show you a baby bird that fell out of its nest. I'm feeding it."

Just before dusk, Bessie said to Celia as she flew out the door with a basket over her arm, "I'll pick the flowers for the dinner tables," for the stress of the day had left her longing to be alone in the fresh mountain air.

In her hunt, she found Tiger and Leopard Lilies on the hill-sides and Daisies and Bleeding Heart in the meadow. Then she ran quickly to a rocky area below where the entrance road came into the property. Japanese Narcissi grew there in clumps, their odor surprisingly strong and sweet for such a tiny flower.

But just as she was about to pick some of the white blossoms, a beaded mocassin appeared right by her hand.

"Ohhh," she said quietly, looking up, her heart beating rapidly. It was the Indian girl, her friend. Bessie stood up, wondering how Indians managed to appear so quickly and so silently. The older girl held out spikes of Mountain Laurel.

"I'm sorry I startled you," she said. "Here, these will make your bouquets more beautiful. The blossoms make good soap, too."

Bessie's eyes widened in amazement, and the girl laughed.

"You're surprised I speak your language?"

"Y-yes! You used sign language before."

"It was better that way. I live in the Miwok tribe about twenty miles beyond Hodgdon's," she said.

"Where did you learn English?"

She leaned against a big yellow pine. "A missionary came into the tribe. His wife taught me. She said, because I learned it quickly and had very little accent, I should go to school below. So my great grandfather, who is Chief, sent me. I went for two years, but...it was lonely. Not every white child is as nice as you."

"I'm real sorry," Bessie said sincerely. "What's your name?"

"In English...Bright Star."

"Mine is Bessie. I get teased sometimes because some people call their cows Bess."

They looked at each other for a second and then both burst out laughing.

"But, I guess I'm stuck with it,' Bessie added, giggling.

"Like my living in a tribe all my life."

"I think it'd be fun being an Indian."

"I like being an Indian," she explained, "but I guess what I'd really like is to be an Indian who has all the good things a white person has."

"My parents have always told me that having good things doesn't make a person happy," Bessie said seriously. "Happiness comes when you are thankful for what you do have."

"You have wise parents. You should go now and I must get through the mountains before it is dark."

The two girls turned to walk east across the meadow.

"The little boy. How is he?" Bessie asked.

"My brother. His leg has mended. He wouldn't go out into the woods with anyone for awhile afterwards without crying."

"It was a scary experience for him, being lost and hurt like that," Bessie nodded.

"We will meet again, Bessie."

Once again the two girls bid goodbye, turning and lifting their arms in salute to each other. With a song in her heart, Bessie walked rapidly back to the hotel.

Dan was waiting at the top of the hill. "People are talking about you and the Indian girl, Bessie. She really is your friend, isn't she?"

"Yes. She really is, Danny. Wanta' help me arrange these bouquets? Woops, be careful with that Mountain Laurel. Bright Star says the blossoms make good soap."

Leslie behaved herself very well around her parents that evening, which was a surprise to all the other children, but when her parents weren't looking, she yanked on Bessie's dress once, almost causing her to spill a bowl of gravy she was setting on the table. And another time, she stuck out her tongue.

"What a brat!" Bessie said under her breath.

Leslie heard her, so when Bessie came near the next time, she whispered, "I'm going to get you for that."

Bessie wasn't afraid, but she decided she had better keep an eye on the insufferable girl from San Francisco.

After dinner was over and the dishes done, Bessie came into the lobby just in time to see Leslie acting strangely. She seemed to be sneaking around, first standing behind a big plant, and then walking rapidly over to a coat rack and standing behind that.

"What in the world!" Bessie muttered, but just then her mother called her to meet some people with whom she was talking.

Later, though, Mrs. Crocker took her aside. "Bessie, do you know what happened to the extra pies I had on the counter in the kitchen? There were five left over from dinner, and I can't find them anywhere. I want to give some to our hired hands."

"No, Mrs. Crocker. Maybe Celia put them in the pantry. I saw them while we were finishing up the dishes."

But, as she was thinking about it, Bessie became suspicious. Could Leslie have...? She looked around, but couldn't find her. Then she snapped her fingers and ran to the church meeting room. Hardly anyone ever went there after dinner. It was a perfect place to hide.

She opened the door slowly, and sure enough! There was Leslie, with her brother and sister, sitting on the floor, stuffing pie into their mouths as fast as they could.

Bessie stood there, unable to make a decision! For one thing, she figured what they had done was stealing. Should she point that out? For another, she didn't think it was probably very good for them to eat so much. Maybe she ought to tell them. She decided on the latter course of action.

"You'll get sick," she said, her voice cutting through the quietness.

Leslie looked up quickly, and, with her mouth full of pie, she sassed, "You'd better not tell, you stupid mountain urchin, with the ugly flour sack dress."

Bessie felt her face turn red. Her dress wasn't made of pretty, expensive material like Leslie's, and it wasn't the latest fashion, maybe, but it was her best one. And it wasn't made out of a flour sack.

She looked down at it. Her sash HAD come loose so it hung down straight, and the patch her mother had put on it did show a little.

In her embarrassment, she didn't know what to say, but Leslie kept talking, pie squishing out of her mouth.

"Called me a brat, you did. I owe you one for that, and if you tell about the pie, I'm going to snatch all your hair off."

Bessie's hand flew up to her head. She didn't much like the idea of losing what little hair she had. Well, there really wasn't any need to tell anyone about the pie. If Mrs. Crocker knew what had happened, and said something, Leslie's parents probably wouldn't ever come back, and that would hurt the Crockers' business.

As it was, the pie snatcher was punished anyway. Even before Bessie could turn to go, Leslie jumped to her feet and, holding her stomach, ran out the door with a look of great distress on her face. Celia told her later that Leslie threw up, as did her sister, and her little brother had a queasy stomach, too.

Bessie was sorry that her tormentor missed the musical program her parents presented that evening. She also was mortified to realize, however, that she wasn't sorry because she would like to have had Leslie ENJOY herself. She was sorry because,

since Leslie had called her a mountain urchin and made fun of her dress and bragged about the family's locomobile, she wanted her to know that her mother was important and could play really well and her father was a wonderful singer. Then she might take all her meanness back.

Leslie's parents finally got her to confess about the pie. Not that she told them because she felt guilty, but because they, not knowing what had caused her illness, guessed, with a wink at each other, that they'd have to take her to the hospital and she'd have to have all kinds of terrible tasting medicine.

The next day after worship service, she had to apologize to Mrs. Crocker. Celia said later that she looked a bit pale when she apologized, and didn't even wave goodbye when they all left after lunch.

As for Bessie, she was glad they were gone, even if she didn't get to see their horseless carriage work. She knew that Celia took a picture of it with the camera her father had given her for her eighteenth birthday. And she knew that Mr. Crocker had decided that if Leslie's parents were going to drive their locomobile on up to Yosemite Valley, he would fine them money for passing by Crocker Station, and they wouldn't be allowed to drive it anywhere in Yosemite Valley itself.

"Those crazy machines frighten the wildlife and the noise ruins the quiet of the countryside," he declared, but he needn't have worried. They went straight back to San Francisco.

But as Thomas told his family later, it wouldn't have done any good to fine them and lay down the law, anyway, because Mr. Crocker didn't own the road, and besides, if one person had a horseless carriage, pretty soon, lots of people would and who could stop that?

What Bessie didn't know was that Leslie would be back in September and would be the cause of one of the most terrible experiences of her life. If she HAD known what was in store for her, she might have hidden away somewhere by herself in the mountains.

Chapter 12
It's Gold!

Summer brought plenty of opportunity for other than lessons and work. Bessie spent most of her free time in the woods by herself. Once Danny invited her to hike with him up to Hodgdon's Station. She was hoping he would agree to going on to the Miwok village, where Bright Star lived, but he was concerned about getting home before dark.

"How did you and Bright Star get to be such good friends, Bessie?"

"I was going to keep it my secret forever, Danny. Promise you won't tell."

"I understand about secrets. I have lots of them. Maybe you can tell me yours and I'll tell you one of mine, and then we'll both promise not to tell anyone else."

"I'll never, never tell your secret until I die," she swore solemnly. "I wouldn't tell you about Bright Star, except I never said I wouldn't."

So as they hiked, she shared the story about how she met Bright Star on Priest's Grade and how she helped her find her little brother, not putting in the part about thinking she was being chased by a bear. Then he shared a few things that were dearest to his heart, although she couldn't figure out why any of them shouldn't be told, like the time he had a dream that he had become a famous doctor.

Nevertheless, she had promised, and she'd keep that promise, for she had been taught since her early years that a person who couldn't keep her word was not to be trusted in anything, and although she wasn't sure that was totally true, the idea was very impressive and probably worth one's efforts.

One unusually warm day Theodora sent her to Crocker's to get the mail. She stopped at Rush Creek on the way, for it seemed especially bubbly and musical that special afternoon. She was about to throw a rock into it when she heard a deep crackly voice behind her.

"Great Spirit make water for fish." She whirled around, startled. Standing there was an old man. Bessie knew immediately who he was: Old Grizzly, chief of the Miwok Indian tribe up near Hodgdon's. She had heard many stories about him, and had seen him from a distance.

He was a "hundred winters old" that year and looked it! His teeth were brown and broken, his hair white and scraggly and his face very crinkly and horribly scarred by numerous scrapes he'd had with Grizzly bears. His clothes were torn and ragged and Bessie, remembering Bright Star's neatness, wasn't sure it was because the tribe was living in poverty or if the chief, at his age, didn't really care how he looked.

Bessie liked him instantly, because he had kind eyes and a friendly smile.

"You must be Mr. Grizzly. You're Bright Star's great Grandfather, aren't you?"

His face lit up like a coal oil lamp.

"Bright Star? You know?"

"Yes. She is my friend."

"Someday you come visit. We take you to Hetch Hetchy Valley. Very beautiful. Great Spirit make special."

"Thank you, Mr. Grizzly, maybe I can do that someday."

In his gnarled hand, he grasped a string of fish which he held out toward her. "Very nice. See? For Henry. Henry Crocker good

man. Present for him."

"I was just going there myself. We can walk together," she smiled. They fell into step, the old man and the young girl, as comfortable as if they had known each other forever. "Mr. Grizzly," she asked, "could you tell me about one of the times you killed a Grizzly bear?" Then she listened, delighted, as he entertained her with one experience after another.

One of the things Bessie wanted to do was improve her gold panning skills. Her Mother gave her a frying pan to use which she had scrubbed thoroughly to remove any grease.

"This step is important, Bessie," her mother explained. "Since gold is heavier than dirt or water, once it is free from the rock in which it is found, it will settle down to the bottom of the pan and lodge there. If there is any grease at all, the gold will slide back into the stream."

The shape of the pan was important, too. Most prospectors used a round one with sloping sides, so her frying pan, even with a long handle on it, was all that was needed.

At first she wasn't very proficient. She could scoop up the

gravel and dirt from the stream bed all right, but she couldn't get the hang of moving the pan around in a circle the right way so the water would slosh out, taking the gravel and dirt with it, and leaving gold behind, assuming there was gold.

It was fun, though, and she kept thinking how wonderful it would be if she could get enough of the precious metal to give to her mother and father as a contribution to the family finances. After all, she was ten years old!

Thus, one day, after going through all the right motions, a prickly thrill went through her when she saw some shiny gold flecks in her pan! Holding it as level as she could, she ran through the trees, calling to her father as she went.

He had stayed at the cabin that morning because he was going below, at noon, with some thumb sized nuggets he'd dug out of an abandoned mine in which he had been working. She found him sharpening his tools.

"Princess!" he boomed, wiping sweat off his forehead and moustache with the big red bandana handkerchief he had in his pocket. She usually felt especially proud to see him use the hanky, because she was the one who always ironed it. But today she scarcely noticed, she was so excited.

"Daddy! Look what I found in the brook!"

He took her find from her and tilted it toward the light.

"Hmmmmm," he said, and then he reached his thumb into the pan and pushed against the colored flecks with his nail.

"It is gold, isn't it, Daddy?" she squealed, impatient because he said nothing. Finally he cleared his throat.

"It's shiny, and it's gold colored, Princess. But, I'm sorry to say, it's not the real stuff. It's actually..." He cleared his throat again, "...pyrite."

"Fool's gold," she murmured, embarrassed. He put his arm around her, giving her a big hug.

"Don't feel badly. There isn't a miner, young or old, that hasn't been tricked by fool's gold at one time or other in his life. Good enough metal of its own, I reckon. Someday someone will find the use for it that the good Lord had in mind when He put it in the ground."

Three days after she found the pyrite, though, a gold colored hunk of something else showed in her frying pan.

She felt it between her fingers. It was about the size of a marble. She poked her fingernail into it, certain it would shatter. Only it didn't! Her heart began to beat rapidly.

She held it carefully in her fingers and walked uphill through the trees. Suddenly she dropped the whatever--it--was, found it again, and continued to walk sedately to where her father and mother were sitting on the back porch, talking. She waited until they gave her permission to interrupt.

"Daddy, this is probably fool's gold, but it doesn't shatter," she said hesitantly, and handed it to him.

He looked at it carefully, poked at it with his nail and then went into the cabin to get his magnifying glass. He began to chuckle. "You found yourself some gold, Princess," he said.

She pressed her hands tightly against her face, because she could feel it was hot. But she couldn't hold it in any longer. With a yell she jumped up and down, clapping her hands, ignoring the fact that her mother liked her always to act like a lady. But Theodora didn't scold. She looked at the gold carefully herself, smiling broadly.

"What do you think it's worth, Thomas?" she asked.

"Can't tell exactly, but I reckon it'll bring, maybe $4.00."

"$4.00!" Bessie squealed. "That's a lot!"

"A day's wages for a miner," he said, nodding his head. "That is a lot of money. Reckon you can find another?"

She didn't need urging. She took off like a jackrabbit, as her father described it, her parents' laughter following her. But there was no more gold for her that day. Still, finding the nugget was all she needed for awhile. And since it was her very first one, her father let her keep it.

Bessie's father and mother had taken to reading the Bible aloud each evening. Sometimes she found it hard to concentrate, and would start yawning.

But one night, she heard Thomas read something about a door and she came awake in a hurry.

"...verily I say unto thee, I am the door of the sheep. All that ever came before me are thieves and robbers: but the sheep did not hear them. I am the door..."

Her father continued to read, but she wasn't listening anymore. She was seeing, in her mind's eye, the preacher who walked out of the church gathering at Crocker's Hotel, shouting, "Walk out...through that prison door!"

She held her lower lip with her upper teeth. If Jesus were the way into the sheep pen, maybe He was the door out of the devil's prison. She sighed, still not understanding. Somehow, some way, there would come a time when the puzzle would come together, she felt certain.

Chapter 13
The Awful Experience

Theodora Waters Quimby was a woman of determination once she set her mind to a course of action. And at this moment, she was forming a plan.

She studied her daughter closely as Bessie lifted the heavy iron from the cookstove and set it gingerly on the skirt of her dress which was freshly laundered. How quickly the time had flown since they had come to the Crocker Station area. Not that the work and social times hadn't been rewarding, but...and she sighed... there had been precious few moments alone with this girl who would soon be a woman.

"Bessie, you're ironing a tuck into the hem. Use a little water and flatten it out."

Yes, she thought, some things are more important than work or helping Mrs. Crocker, and with Thomas planning to be gone a good part of the summer, it was time she corrected that. She stood up to the full height of her small frame.

"Finish your ironing quickly, Bessie. You and I are going on a tramp. I'll pack a lunch. You get your fishing pole. Well, now, you'll be burning your dress if you stand there and gawk at me," Theodora remonstrated. "Keep your wits about you, please."

So it was that mother and daughter spent many fun packed days picking berries, picnicking, hiking, and fishing.

Bessie also panned more gold, for the chore had become easier for her each time she went. There were no more nuggets but there was "color" in her pan.

When Danny looked at it, he smiled. "Gold dust. My father says, when he was a young man, he used to sell it to buy groceries."

Bessie giggled. "We use it to buy groceries now! I think of it as ground up nuggets."

Danny laughed and then said seriously, "This looks pretty high grade to me."

Bessie smiled shyly, pleased that he had told her, in a round about way, that she had done a good job.

Soft as a hush the first rain fell after September began. Bessie walked to Crocker's, her face turned up toward the sky, loving the cool wetness of it.

But the walk back home became an agitated trot, for, as she told her mother, "There's a nasty storm coming to Crocker Station."

"Whatever are you talking about?" her mother said as she heated a big black iron pot of soup on the cookstove.

"Leslie Blackman. Celia says she's coming tomorrow with her parents AND brother and sister. Ugh!"

"Bessie," her mother admonished, "I can't believe you are talking like that. Shame."

"But Mother, Celia is going to be in San Francisco and won't be able to entertain them. Mrs. Crocker expects ME to do it. By myself!"

If the guest had been anyone else, she would have felt very honored AND very important. After all, who but Mrs. Crocker would trust a ten year old girl with a big job like that? But she had a feeling in the pit of her stomach that it was going to mean trouble. There was no getting around it, though. So the next day she presented herself with a forced smile to Mrs. Crocker.

She and Leslie didn't start off well at all. First thing, Leslie was bossy, as before. And she made fun of Bessie's clothes again. To top it off, she became very demanding.

"Mrs. Crocker told me you found some gold this summer. Let me see it."

"My father put it in the bank."

"Then let's go find some more!"

"It's not easy work, Leslie, and it takes lots of time. Besides it's pretty wet in the forest, and not too warm. I don't think you'd like it much."

"You just don't want us to find any gold like you did, because then you wouldn't have anything to brag about. Now, TAKE US GOLD HUNTING!"

"YEAAAA!" sassed Jan and Tad, her sister and brother.

Bessie's stomach began to churn, but she shrugged. If they wanted to go look for gold, then, she'd take them to look for gold.

"You'll need different clothes because you'll get muddy. And I'm NOT saying we can find any gold."

"We'll find some," Leslie said. "And we DON'T need any different clothes. My father will buy me a hundred outfits like this, anytime I ask.

So, after borrowing some panning materials from the Crocker Station shed, Bessie started out, walking fast like she usually did. The three of them trailed after her.

"Slow down, Urchin," Leslie whined as she tried to climb over a fallen log, but finally giving up and going around the end.

Bessie looked over her shoulder as she walked and said, "Leslie, my name is Bessie, not Urchin."

"My name is Besssss-ee-eee!" Leslie mocked.

Jan and Tad took it up and they started chanting, "Besssss-ee-eee! Besssss-ee-eee!"

Then Leslie sneered, "They name cows Bess. Moooooo!"

Bessie wanted to say something mean, but, for one thing, she didn't know what to say. For another, her mother had always told her, "When people aren't being nice, don't lower yourself to their level by answering back, Bessie."

So she said nothing, pointing instead to a little patch of Indian Paint Brush, with its fiery orange flowers.

"Oh, let's pick some!" Jan squealed, and they squatted down immediately, grabbing the flowers roughly.

"Be careful," Bessie warned. "You're pulling some of the plants out of the ground. They won't grow again next year."

"So what, Urchin?' Leslie growled. "But who cares about stupid flowers anyway? Let's get on with hunting for gold."

Walking down a gentle slope, cutting through the forest, and continuing until they came to Rush Creek only took five minutes. Bessie led them past the deep pools under the bluffs and in the bends, seeking out long shallow ribbons of water which flowed over fine sand and rock.

"Now, watch," Bessie said. "You fill your pan with gravel, and..."

"That's not the way you do it," Leslie retorted. "I know, because I read a book on it once."

"Then do it your own way," Bessie said.

Leslie tried, but the gravel constantly slushed out of the pan, leaving nothing behind. All of a sudden, though, she let out a screech.

"GOLD! GOLD! I've found some. I've found gold! And this is the BEST gold! Lots better than yours, Urchin," she shrieked.

She and her brother and sister began to dance around like they didn't have any sense at all, in Bessie's opinion. She looked in Leslie's pan. "This isn't real gold, Leslie."

"It is, too! You're just jealous."

"It's pyrite," Bessie said quietly. "Known as fool's gold."

"You calling me a fool, you fool?"

"No, Leslie. That's what the miners call this kind of metal. Real gold isn't that shiny. Besides, if I press my fingernail into it, it shatters, see? Gold doesn't do that."

Leslie grabbed her pan away in a temper, and looked at it very carefully. Then, without a word, she started panning again. This time they went at it seriously, and seemed to be unaware of anything or anybody else.

What happened soon after that turned Bessie's day into a nightmare. She was sitting on a rock, watching them pan, when all of a sudden she saw a flash of something fuzzy and brown which disappeared into the forest at an angle downhill. A naturally curious girl, she glanced at Leslie and the others.

Satisfied that they seemed completely absorbed in what they were doing, she walked rapidly in the direction of the unknown creature, intending to keep the gold panners within sight.

Suddenly she heard behind her, "WHOOP WHOOP WHOOP!" Her charges were following at a rapid pace. Turning, Bessie ran to meet them.

"We're going back, now," she commanded.

"NO!" Leslie sassed.

"Mrs. Crocker has a rule. We aren't to go beyond that stand of yellow pine."

"Then why did YOU?"

"The rule isn't for me. Look, I'm used to the woods. But you could get hurt. Come on. We have to go back."

"That's silly nonsense," Leslie said and marched right on, with Jan and Tad following along like two shadows. "If a little baby urchin like you is safe in the woods," she shot over her shoulder, "then CERTAINLY I am, too. You saw something and I'm going to find out what it was. You can't hide it from me!"

"Leslie!" Bessie yelled, and then in her frustration, she added, "You're...you're not a very nice girl AT ALL!"

By the time she caught up with them, the brook which, at this junction, ran deeper, had curved around and lay straight ahead.

Leslie looked over her shoulder as she walked on. "So THAT'S it, is it? Here's where you found your gold, and you didn't want us to know about it. You're the selfish one, aren't you?"

"Watch out!" Bessie warned, but just as she did, Leslie stepped onto the edge of the bank, so soggy from the recent rain that it chunked off.

She screamed as she slipped, her feet going straight out from under her. Bessie ran to help, but Leslie slid right down the wet bank and into the icy cold water.

It was only about a foot deep, but one would have thought it was eight feet, the way she screamed and hollered. "I'M GOING TO DROWN! HELP!" she yowled.

When she saw she wasn't drowning, she stood up in the water and squawked, "MY DRESS! MY LOVELY NEW DRESS! IT'S RUINED!"

Bessie, as well as Jan and Tad, tried to pull her up the bank to the top, but she was so much heavier, it worked just the opposite, and soon all four were in the stream, wet, muddy and cold.

Somehow everyone scrambled out, and began the trudge back up the hill and through the forest, with all but Bessie bawling about their misfortune. When they reached the bottom of Crocker's meadow, they raised their voices several decibels, so a handful of folks came running out of the hotel to see what was wrong. The children's mother came flying down the hill to meet them.

As soon as she got within twenty feet of them, Leslie pointed at Bessie and howled, "SHE did it! Bessie pushed us! Right over the bank and into the river!"

"The river!" her mother gasped, frowning and looking wildly at the accused. "What river?"

All three children began with their own loud version of the story, while Bessie simply stood there, shocked into silence.

"We'll get to the bottom of this," Mrs. Blackman said, glaring at Bessie, and herding her offspring back to the hotel. Bessie trailed behind them, and by the time she got there, her own

mother and Mrs. Crocker had rushed out into the little crowd that had gathered around. Leslie, thoroughly enjoying the attention, pointed at Bessie again and told her story.

Theodora looked at her daughter sternly and said, in a firm, no nonsense voice, "Bessie, go to the kitchen immediately." Everyone heard her, Bessie was sure, so while they oh'd and ah'd over the city kids and their muddy clothes, she trudged off, totally humiliated.

She was angry, too. She always tried to tell the truth, and since Leslie had out and out lied, she felt that her mother should have, at least, asked about her side of the story.

"She believed that brat," she sniffed to herself as she shuffled along, water squishing from her boots, leaving wet prints on the floor. "And everybody else will think I'm terrible."

She stood in the kitchen for a moment, not knowing what to do. Just then she heard someone coming. Not wanting to face anyone, she grabbed the handle of the nearest door and yanked it open. The broom closet! She stepped inside and closed the door.

Just as the dark closed in around her, she heard her mother's voice, calling. She wasn't in the habit of disobeying, but this time, she didn't answer. She could hear her mother leave, so she sank down to the floor. A mop dangled damply in her face. She brushed it aside angrily, and it tumbled off the wall, making a clatter and giving her a sharp bump on the forehead.

The tears flowed silently as she vowed to stay in the broom

closet forever! She'd DIE there, she decided, and then they'd all be sorry. Or maybe...maybe she would steal some food from the kitchen and go out to live in the forest all by herself.

"I'll NEVER EVER come back, either," she stated emphatically.

But just as she was figuring out how she could manage that, the closet door opened. And there was Theodora. Bessie blinked up at her, and then looked away. Even if her mother didn't spank her, Bessie decided, she would never forgive her for thinking such bad things about her. Never!

Then she felt a hand on her shoulder and a loving voice spoke into her ear. "Bessie, it's all right. I knew you didn't push those children."

"You knew?" she squeaked through her tears. "Then why...?"

"I was trying to calm everyone down. It seemed best to get you out of the way."

"But now everyone thinks I'm bad," she choked out.

"No, they don't. But I apologize. It wasn't a very good decision."

Apologize? Her mother? Her mother never apologized for any-thing! At least not to Bessie. Had she heard right? She turned to look into the beautiful soft eyes which were level with hers. Suddenly, she was in her mother's arms sobbing. That, in itself, was most unusual. Her mother, who was hugging her tightly, was not the hugging type, and certainly Bessie seldom cried in her presence, for self control was considered of prime importance.

Theodora spoke softly. "Leslie's little brother soon told the whole story. Mrs. Blackman wants Leslie to apologize to you."

Bessie took a deep breath and let it out, relieved, but she said, "I don't want to see her ever again."

"It's important to forgive, Bessie. Otherwise, you can carry bad feelings inside all your life, and that isn't good for you.

"Come, Dear, we'll go wash up and comb your hair. Mrs. Crocker found an old dress of Celia's. It's clean and quite pretty, and I think it will fit you all right. We'll borrow it for awhile. It'll make you feel better."

So Bessie fixed up, and Leslie said she was sorry, although Bessie felt sure she didn't mean it.

Chapter 14
Tripsy Says Goodbye

Bessie loved Tripsy so intensely that she sometimes felt she couldn't live if something happened to her. Her parents would look at each other knowingly, but neither had the heart to suggest she do what was right for the animal. It took Danny to educate her.

"Pet deer are just wild animals, Bessie," he had told her. "They need to be in their natural environment away from humans. They can never be completely happy otherwise."

So Bessie, even though it saddened her, began to take her charge into the woods to get her used to them, going farther and farther each time. At times she purposely would chase the little deer so she'd be afraid of people a little bit and not be an easy target for a hunter. Tripsy thought it was a game, though, so she never ran far. She'd peek around the trees and start wandering back.

Gradually the young doe began to feel comfortable in her natural environment and didn't return as readily.

The first night she didn't come home, her mistress couldn't

sleep at all, worrying about her. But she was back at the cabin the next morning. Bessie hugged and kissed her, which she didn't like much, but she put up with it, nosing around for a handful of sugar.

One day while they were walking through the woods together, Tripsy suddenly sniffed the air, reeled around and raced off through the woods like lightning. Bessie laid low behind a big log, wondering what had spooked her.

Then she saw them: Two old prospectors sauntering through the trees, their mules loaded down with supplies. They had come up from Tioga Road and were cutting across the Quimby prop-

erty, heading up the mountain at a slant. At the angle they were traveling, they would pass fairly close to her. She pressed down into the brush behind a big log, watching carefully.

As they drew nearer, they stopped to check their gear, Bessie felt a stab of fear, for she recognized these men: Jack Gaston and his sidekick, Maxie, Old Long Nose and Spitter themselves, the ones who had threatened her father, the ones who had shot Tripsy's mother. Holding her breath, she stayed hidden, watching until they were out of sight, hoping that Tripsy, wherever she was, would keep right on moving.

As it was, when Tripsy was full grown, she stayed away for longer periods and finally, she didn't show up at all. Bessie would see her in the forest, sometimes, and she usually came when she was called.

Now that the Crockers knew Theodora could play the piano so beautifully, and Thomas could sing, they frequently invited them to entertain guests, so if Thomas was back in time from the mines or from one of his trips, the Quimbys would go early enough to help serve, and would take their evening meal there.

At Mrs. Crocker's urging, Theodora began to teach music to both Celia and Johnny. Celia was extremely interested, and Johnny showed real talent but Bessie's progress seemed to be met with little success. The Crockers wished to pay for the tutoring, but Theodora was uncomfortable with that thought, so she came up with an idea!

"How would it be, Mrs. Crocker, if we were to set up a regular school for all the children in the area, those whose parents work for you, and Johnny and Bessie, of course. You could pay me for teaching the school and then you wouldn't mind my giving Celia and Johnny music lessons on the side without pay." Mrs. Crocker was so delighted, having taught school in the past herself, that she had it all set up the following week in one of their cabins.

Theodora received $20 a month for her work, which supplemented the family income considerably, since Thomas still wasn't finding much gold.

It wasn't a proper school, of course, because they didn't have

regular books or blackboards and other items that regular schools had. Class was five days a week, starting at 10:00, continuing until noon and commencing again at 2:30. Once in awhile, Theodora went below, usually to Groveland or Big Oak Flat with Thomas, so there wouldn't be any school at all for a day or so, but no one minded that.

Study time, chores and playtime were after lunch and in the late afternoon. Bessie loved the lessons and the studying. It seemed she just couldn't get enough to satisfy her.

Theodora had sent for some new study books, which would have to come by stage. The children awaited them as eagerly as the adults awaited letters from friends and relatives. But because of heavy snows that fell, the stage couldn't get through. So finally, Danny went to Coulterville on snowshoes and picked them up at the postoffice there.

The children danced around him in delight when he returned. He was the hero of the day, and basked in the attention modestly, as usual. Among other letters he passed out, there were five from Thomas to Theodora, for he had gotten temporary work in Sonora. Thomas also had written one to Bessie, which she read and reread eight times before the day was out.

After the letters had been given out, the children were still waiting. Danny had hidden the package of study books at first, pretending he knew nothing about them, but at last he presented them, and the boys and girls went crazy with excitement, running everywhere showing them to anyone who would look.

"Someday," Bessie thought, "someday I'll go to a real school with a whole bunch of children, where I can be there all day and learn everything in the world."

Chapter 15
The Unusual Christmas

Although there was nothing unusual or luxurious about it, the cabin was perfectly designed for the Quimbys' needs. They had settled in very comfortably, ready for anything winter sent their way.

On Christmas Eve day, a snow that fell like a whisper covered everything in sight, ushering in a quiet stillness that spoke peace to the heart. Like a soft, warm blanket it made the Quimby property look like a fairyland in white.

Exciting plans had already been made. They had helped the Crockers decorate the hotel dining room with boughs and berries two days before, and baked with them, the idea being that they would all spend Christmas Eve together.

About noon, their plans were changed, for a storm swept into the area with a fierceness that sent Bessie scurrying to close the woodshed door. Her scarf was pulled into the rushing air which swished it up and away from the woodshed, so she scampered out to get it and found herself barely able to stand.

The gale became full of sleet that blinded her eyes and stung her face. She cried out, but the roar of the storm stole her voice, throwing it into the air to join the moaning and crying of the wind.

"Where's the cabin?" she wondered frantically, "I can't see it."

The wind pushed her against her will, slamming her up against a tree, only to pull her away again. Suddenly she bumped against something soft. A cry burst from her throat. Then recognition came and she encircled a long wet hairy neck with her arms.

"Tripsy! Oh, Tripsy. You've come back for shelter. Take me to the cabin, Tripsy. Help me!"

As if the doe understood, she fought against the wind, dragging the weight of her little friend, until at last, she entered the woodshed. Bessie continued to hold on to her, crying, while Tripsy walked to the hay which was piled in a corner, always there for her use should she want it.

The child pushed open the kitchen door where her father was polishing his boots. He looked up with alarm, for she was soaking wet and close to hysteria. He picked her up in his arms and called for Theodora as he carried her to the potbellied stove.

"Daddy, Tripsy saved me. She's in the woodshed. I couldn't get the door shut."

"I'll take care of that, Princess, and I'll rub Tripsy down. Your mother will get you into some dry clothes and put some hot water in the tub for your feet. You can tell us what happened later."

Although she was bitterly disappointed to have missed Christmas with the Crockers, Bessie felt afterwards that the storm was the best thing that could have happened to them for, as they sat around the potbellied stove, which glowed red from the fire within, she learned some surprising facts.

She nearly fell off her stool, for instance, when her father said suddenly, "You had two brothers and a sister, you know, Bessie. Mother never was able to carry a baby until..."

"Thomas..." Theodora protested.

"She needs to know some of the facts of life, Dear. She's almost eleven, and very grownup for her age. Anyway, as I was saying, you do know where babies come from, Princess, don't you?"

"Thomas!" Mother protested again, her voice stronger this time.

But Bessie spoke up. "Of course. Celia has taught me a lot of things, and I've seen ladies with babies in their tummies. It's God's way of keeping the baby safe until it can make its own way in the world. Like Tripsy. She was safe until she was born and her mother was shot."

"Yes. Well, the boys never lived to be born, and your sister lived just a few hours."

"I had to stay in bed nine months when I had you, young lady," Mother added, a bit embarrassed, but wanting to join in. "The doctor insisted. And you'll never guess where you entered the world."

"San Francisco?" Bessie asked.

"No. That's where you were supposed to be born, but instead, it was Big Oak Flat."

"Big Oak Flat!" she exclaimed.

"Yes, not far from Priest's Hotel," her father replied. "Your

mother was planning on going to Stockton, and then continue by boat to San Francisco when it was time. We started out with that in mind, borrowing a wagon and making a bed in the back of it. I wanted her to be warm and as comfortable as possible. It was in the dead of winter, like now only, of course, it was February. We had borrowed a four horse team, but it was so slick, they had trouble keeping their footing.

"The discouraging thing was, right out in the middle of nowhere, the wagon broke down. I had tools with me, but it took hours to fix it, using up most of our daylight.

"But we started again, and eventually the roads became so bad and the wagon we were in was so bumpy, you decided you'd had enough jiggling up and down! So guess what?"

Bessie whispered, "What?"

"You let your mother know that you were coming out!"

Theodora took up the story. "I didn't want you to be born in an open wagon on a bitterly cold day in the wilderness. There would be no way to take care of you, and you might die!"

Thomas reached for his wife's hand. "Or, your mother might have died," he said solemnly. "But there was no place for you to be born!"

"Like Jesus," Bessie murmured out loud.

"That's right, Princess!" her father said, admiringly. Did you know..." he said, leaning his arms on his knees and clasping his hands together, "...that the inns in His day weren't like the hotels we have now? They were shaped a bit like a U, with small open rooms around the sides and end. In the center was a courtyard with a well in it, and hay for animals. Travelers could stop there free of charge, feed and water their animals, and then, if one of the open rooms were available, they could sleep there. When Joseph and Mary arrived at one of those resting places, there wasn't a room left, because...do you remember, Princess?"

"Yes," she nodded wide-eyed, "because lots of people were coming to Bethlehem to be taxed and they'd gotten there first. So Joseph and Mary had to sleep in a stable. It was like the little stable the Crockers have setting on their table with figures they put in it."

"No. I don't think so, Princess. For one thing, in Israel, wood was scarce. Adobe and rocks were used for building. Caves were a perfect place for nomads and shepherds to keep their animals: cattle, sheep, maybe camels. It's more likely that Joseph found a cave, and that's where the Lord was born."

"The animals must have been surprised!" Bessie laughed.

Her father laughed, too. "They probably put up a howl all right. MOOOOOOO, BAAAAAAA, EE-AW, EE-AW, EE-AW. No doubt Joseph even built a fire, and made a pot of soup over it."

Bessie, still giggling over her father's rendition of surprised animals added, "Then Jesus was born and they wrapped him up and put him in a manger."

"Yes. So, you were right, Bessie girl. Your birth was a lot like that of Jesus."

"That makes you more special than we ever dreamed, Bessie," her mother said, smiling warmly.

"O Little Town of Bethlehem," her father began in his lovely, soft tenor voice, and soon all three were singing Christmas carols, one right after the other. Bessie hugged herself in her mind, thinking about it all, and how nice it was to be where they were, and wondered if Tripsy understood anything about Christmas. She'd have to go out into the woodshed before bedtime and explain it all to her.

Her father pumped up the coal oil lamp, so it would keep shining brightly, and suddenly, the love Bessie felt for her mother and father welled up in her heart until she could barely breathe.

Her eyes shining, she asked, "So if we were out in the middle of the forest, with no place to go, and I was telling you that I wanted to get out into the world, how did I get born in Big Oak Flat?"

"Ah, Princess, that's the best part of the story. You see, your mother had begun to cry, because, remember, she had lost three babies already, and she wanted you so badly. And nothing was working out like we planned."

Theodora spoke up. "Your father stopped the team, climbed back into the wagon where I was, and prayed. He asked the Lord to please let us have you, healthy and strong, and to keep me from dying. And then he started the team going again."

Bessie was leaning forward, fascinated.

Mother spoke next. "It was dark by then, and after what seemed like forever, I heard your father shout, 'There it is, Theodora! There it is!' I pulled myself up with difficulty and looked. Lights! There were lights ahead! I started laughing and crying at the same time, realizing that we had made it as far as Groveland."

"But our troubles weren't over," Thomas continued. "We didn't know anyone in Groveland at that time. We knew, too, that there was no doctor there. But I had decided I would stop at the nearest place where there was a light burning to see if someone would give us shelter and find a midwife for us. Just then your mother cried out, 'Thomas, hurry!' knowing you were about to be born. That frightened me, so I cracked the whip over the horses' heads and they raced down the main street. The buildings were all dark because businesses had closed up for the day, you see.

"And then, the strangest thing happened. Just ahead, in the center of the street, there stood a shadowy figure. He was waving his arms, and as we slowed down, I could see he was an old Chinese man. He pointed down the street ahead of us and shouted, 'BIG OAK FLAT! WHITE HOUSE!'

"Big Oak Flat was two miles further. Why I decided to trust the direction of an old man who hadn't the slightest idea who we were or why we were there, I don't know. But, for some reason, I urged our tired horses on up the mountain and soon we were pulling into Big Oak Flat.

The first building we saw was a big white house, a two story affair, and when I pulled the team to a halt, the door opened. There, in the door, stood a woman.

" 'MY WIFE,' I shouted. 'SHE'S HAVING A BABY!'

"She whirled around, yelling for a man who came running out. They bustled us into a nice, warm bedroom next to the kitchen, and the man said, 'Ordinarily there is no doctor in this town. But there happens to be one visiting. He's staying at the hotel.' Can you imagine that, Princess? A doctor just visiting, in the middle of winter!

"He hitched up his horse and sleigh and we dashed off through the forest.

"'A short cut!' he shouted, and soon we were running into the hotel yelling, 'We need the doctor! It's an emergency!'

"The desk clerk looked at us over his glasses and said, 'The doctor has retired for the night. He is not to be disturbed.'

"'Give me that register!' my host yelled, ignoring the protests of the clerk. He found the doctor's room number and was up those stairs banging on his door in two seconds. The doc came running, putting his pants and coat on as we went. By the time we got back to the house, the lady was rubbing your mother's hands and feet, trying to get her warm."

"Yes," Theodora nodded, "I had been shivering, so she had fixed hot tea for me to drink, and put hot bricks, all wrapped up in towels, all over me. It was the busiest room you ever saw!"

Bessie laughed in delight as she listened.

Her mother laughed, too. "Your father was trying to tell the doctor my history of losing children, and the doctor was trying to tell your father to keep quiet and do what he was told, and everyone was talking at once. Finally he shooed everybody out and you were born, healthy and strong."

"You know what, Princess?" Thomas said. "The next day, after you were born, I went back to Groveland, looking for the Chinese man who pointed the way, so I could thank him, and I was told by person after person that NO old Chinese man lived in that town or Big Oak Flat. Some young Chinese, yes. But old? No."

Bessie felt chills go right up her spine and into her hair. "It was all a miracle!" she breathed. "The Chinese man, the people in the house and the doctor. A real miracle."

They didn't talk a lot after that. There was too much to think about. But, as Bessie was telling Celia later, "I've NEVER EVER had such a wonderful Christmas in my whole life!"

97

Chapter 16
Well, Hello, Tripsy!

Bessie had only two dresses all winter, both the same color, for her mother would never think of putting her in anything but blue. For all her determination not to encourage vanity, Theodora did allow herself the luxury of making certain that her daughter's enormous blue eyes were emphasized. They were the child's best feature, in her estimation, and thus should be shown to best advantage.

But since the blue was faded and the little rips and tears were becoming more numerous, and there was no money for material for a new one, Mrs. Crocker offered to buy a dress for Bessie. However, Theodora was so mortified, that the offer was never mentioned again. Taking charity was strictly forbidden in the Quimby family.

Theodora said, "There's no disgrace in not having new and expensive clothes, Bessie. The disgrace comes when you take from others and don't work for what you get. Always remember that."

However, when the 23rd of February came, along with Bessie's eleventh birthday, she found, on her breakfast plate, a plain brown paper package. She looked at it for such a long time that her mother laughed, "Aren't you going to open it?"

Bessie didn't want to touch it, let alone open it, for it was too wonderful and totally unexpected. Presents were far between, and she had only received a few in her lifetime.

So she held her dish of oatmeal in her hands and ate it carefully down to the last bite. When she was finished, she reached for the package and slowly pulled the wrapping off.

"Ohhh," she said softly, and then looked up, distress in her eyes. "Mother, you've cut down your only summer dress for me. What will you wear now? I'll feel guilty everytime I put it on."

"I'm glad I had it to make over into a dress for you. You aren't to wear it until spring and the air has warmed a bit, and then only for good. Perhaps by then, I'll be able to make a new one for myself. Who knows?"

April, with its breathless beauty, had almost slipped away when Bessie received one of the biggest surprises of her life. It happened on a bright, sunshiny morning when she was at her creek, lying on her stomach on a big flat rock, hanging her head and arms over the edge, looking at the water sparkling by.

She tried to mimic its sounds, but couldn't. Nothing, in her estimation, could sound as beautiful as her mountain brook. Sometimes she pretended it was calling to her. "Bessie Ploop!" it would gurgle, in her imagination. "Bessie Ploop. Bessie Plop! Splash, Bessie Quimby, glop, gurple, splash!"

She watched it bubble its way through the rocks and trees in the thick forest. The REALLY nice thing about a brook, she decided, is that it can leave you but still stay where you are! Should she take off her shoes and stand on the little sandbar so the water could wash over her feet?

She thought for a moment and then answered herself with a "No." A few patches of snow still covered the pine needles above the north bank. The water would be so cold it would make her toes numb. She came to the conclusion that wading probably wasn't the brightest idea she'd had that morning. The year before, when she was ten, she probably would have done it. But now she prided herself on being more grownup and inclined to think things through better.

Instead, she stretched for a roundish, grey black rock in the riffles and turned it over.

"You're perfect!"

And sure enough! On its underside, snuggled against some gray green moss, was a periwinkle!

"Hi, little periwinkle," she laughed, picking it off carefully and holding it in her hand for inspection. It looked like a little pile of pebbles and gravel, but she knew that a little snail was inside and the tiny rocks were his little house.

Suddenly, brush crackled! Yanking her head up, she saw something move.

"What was that?" she breathed to herself silently and then held very still. The area across the brook was thick with timber that marched its way, like a giant army, across the mountains. But there was a break in it, a small clearing that started at the stream and fanned out like a green lollipop, pushing the big trees back. Something had moved over there.

As she watched carefully, a flash of tan shot into a clearing! And then another!

"Ohhhhh," she gasped. "Two little fawn. Twins!" And then she stared hard. "Is that a...tan cross...on one of those babies? No. It couldn't be!" She had to find out!

"Tripsy," she sang high and gently. "Tripsy!"

The fawn stopped right in their tracks and turned their big soft eyes downhill toward her. They were tiny, no more than two and a half feet tall, with little white spots, like flecks of bright sunlight on their backs and tan sides, spots that they would lose by fall, as they grew bigger; spots which served as camouflage for the little animals to protect them from their enemies. One of them sniffed the air.

"Tripsy!" Bessie called again.

Without another sniff, both little deer reeled around and bounded out of sight. Everything was quiet again, but Bessie kept watching, not moving.

Suddenly, brush crackled again. She held her breath. And then she laughed, because out popped Tripsy, right across the stream, looking at her.

"So they are your fawn, Tripsy," she laughed, delighted. "I wish you'd bring them closer."

She held out her hand, "Come see me, Tripsy. It's been a long time since you've been around."

With a whirl, the deer dove into the brush. Bessie scrambled for some brush herself, making sure she was covered. If Tripsy were afraid, maybe she had to be, too.

"Maybe old Long Nose is nosing around again," she said, and then laughed at her own humor. Nevertheless, she checked quickly to be sure there was a way of escape if she had to run. She waited for maybe ten minutes, but didn't see anything. She slipped out of the brush and sat on the flat rock again, waiting. Finally the crackling came again and Tripsy was there, this time with the two little fawn right behind her, keeping their eyes turned in Bessie's direction. "Oh, Tripsy, you've brought them closer for me to see. They're beautiful!"

She watched them breathlessly. Assured that she wasn't an enemy, the fawn began to play again, racing into the clearing. Tripsy joined them. They kicked and jumped and raced around so much Bessie wanted more than anything to do it with them. Giggling, she ran downstream to a fallen log, and balancing herself, balanced her way across it, but Tripsy sent her babies racing for cover by raising her white tail straight up.

"Oh, Tripsy, you KNOW I won't hurt them!" Bessie wailed. "You were teeny when we took you in, don't you remember?"

Tripsy walked downhill toward her, and before long was nibbling some grass from her hand.

"I'd be awfully good to your children, you know that," she said, scratching behind the doe's long pointed ears. Tripsy nosed Bessie's cheek, turned and walked away. Just before she disappeared into the brush, she swung her head around gracefully and looked at her former mistress. Then, she was gone.

Well, Tripsy and her fawn would be better off left alone, Bessie decided. She went back to the brook. So much of her life was centered around it. She had caught fish there. Rainbow trout and the native browns. The rainbows were the prettiest. They had beautiful colors in stripes on their sides...pink, green, blue, yellowish and lavender sometimes.

Just as pretty were the flowers which were beginning to pop up near a rock, or out of a patch of unmelted snow. The buttercups were the brightest, their yellow warming the heart as sunshine does after a storm.

Bessie bunched her dress up in front, forming a big loose pocket and laid the flowers carefully in it. They almost spilled, though, when she saw the shooting stars.

"Ohhhh!" she gasped, dropping to her knees. There were at least twenty of them in a lovely sheltered spot, nestled in a bed of grass. Her father called the flowers birdbills. Her mother preferred the name Cowslips. But shooting star was Bessie's favorite for them. She held one of the purplish red flowers and looked into its yellow face, laughing at its black pointed nose. What a rare treat!

When she had her apron full, she trudged slowly through the forest, her treasures as well as the special time with Tripsy, filling her heart full.

Chapter 17

The Hunter and Tripsy

Thomas came home from one of his long trips that evening, and when Bessie saw him, she ran all the way down the hill to jump into his big arms. He whirled her around and around and both of them chattered and laughed all the way to the cabin.

That night, after it had been suggested that she go to bed, he and Theodora sat by the potbellied stove and talked. Since her door was open a crack, Bessie could hear most of what they were saying and her bed was situated so she could see a little, too.

Her father was sitting with his head in his hands and his elbows on his knees, looking very discouraged.

"I don't know, Theodora. I just don't know. I want so much to be able to buy you and Bessie a few nice things. Why should she have to wear your dresses cut down to her size? And you've always wanted us to have a carriage and a team of our own. I can't even give you that!"

"Oh, Thomas," she said softly, "dear Thomas, it doesn't matter. Wants aren't necessities. We do just fine! We've never asked a nickel of anyone. And we have plenty of food. A roof over our heads, too. Who needs more than that?"

He stood up and began to pace. "If only I could get a strike!" He paused to run his fingers through his hair. "Maybe I ought to try for a job in San Francisco. They're hiring hands on the loading dock for the big boats. It isn't much pay, but at least you'd be in the City. You've always liked it there."

If Bessie had been standing up, she felt, her heart would have sunk right down to her toes. If they had to move to San Francisco, she'd DIE! Just die. This was their home, not San Francisco! If they went to San Francisco, she would never see her little brook again, or Tripsy. Celia and Johnny would miss her. Danny, too. And she might have to see Leslie again because that's where she lived. No, they just COULDN'T go to San Francisco!

And before she thought, she slipped to the door and called out to them, "I have an idea, Daddy!"

There was complete silence as they both jerked around and stared at her.

She stepped out into the room in her nightgown and began to talk fast before her mother could order her back to bed.

"Daddy, while you were gone, I panned on our creek, and found quite a lot of gold dust. And...and I have my gold nugget... and you know how a person, when they find a lot of gold dust, starts poking holes in the banks and works his way up into the mountain to see if there's more gold up above? Well, I've been thinking. Maybe there IS a lot of gold, right here on our own mountain. Maybe you could look for awhile until you find it!"

Her heart was beating very hard, not knowing how they would respond, since they were doing nothing but staring at her. Slowly, still not speaking, they looked at each other.

Then Thomas spoke very quietly, "You know, Theodora, I never thought of the possibility of gold being right here on our own place. Bessie's right. That gold dust has to be coming from somewhere up above. Maybe..."

He turned to his daughter, his eyes wide.

"Thank you, Princess. You'd better get to sleep now. You and I are going to do some heavy prospecting tomorrow."

Bessie shut the door and jumped into bed, happy and sad, all at the same time. She was happy because she'd had a good idea. But sad, because they might not find the gold. So she lay awake a long time that night, trying hard to make the gold happen by imagining every place it might be.

The next morning, she hopped out onto the cold floor, pulled her clothes on fast and rushed into the kitchen where the coffee was bubbling and the delicious smell of cinnamon rolls and fried eggs greeted her.

She moved about at such a fast rate, setting the table and scrubbing the cooking utensils that her mother said, "Slow down, Bessie. The mountain isn't going anywhere."

After they had eaten, Bessie and her father hiked upstream, where they stopped to pan.

After a bit, he said, "We're finding gold flecks, Princess, but not enough. Let's move on up. You never know where the vein will show up. We'll have to work this entire stream to see which direction we should move."

And suddenly Bessie felt terribly grown up. Her father was working the entire stream because of what she had suggested! Furthermore, he was speaking to her as if she were an adult! She was so excited, she doubled her efforts.

They labored all that day. And the next. And the next.

Then Thomas had to go down to Chinese Camp to meet with a man with whom he would travel to Arizona to see a mine.

"Why don't you take the day off, Princess?" he suggested. "Then tomorrow you can start in again. I'm counting on you to keep working until I get back." He tussled her hair with his hand and wrapped a big smile around her. She knew he might not be back for over a week, but she would do everything she could to find the gold that would keep them from moving.

But a day off would be nice, she decided, especially since she had heard that Leslie and her family had come to Crocker's again and she didn't want to be around in case Mrs. Crocker decided she should come down to entertain them. She would go on a hike!

"I would feel better if you took Danny along, Bessie," her mother added. "It's never wise to hike far in the mountains alone. I'm going to Crocker's in a few minutes, so I can suggest it."

By the time Bessie had the lunch packed, Danny was there, grateful to have an excuse to get away for the afternoon. After some discussion, they decided to head up the draw beyond the cabin. There was a beautiful feathery waterfall above which Bessie liked to visit.

Because the water dropped off the mountain from a spring, the pools weren't deep nor the water swift, except in midwinter. She'd never been there in the deep snow, because she didn't have snowshoes that fit her, although she secretly hoped her father would make some for her someday.

She also hoped that he would think of making her some skis, too, because then, when the stage wasn't running and her parents had to go below, she could ski with them. Even if she'd had snowshoes and skiis, though, she knew she wouldn't have gone into the mountains in winter alone. As her father always said to her, "The mountains will treat you well, Princess, as long as you respect them. So use good sense when you're in them and don't take chances."

She believed that and was careful, even on a nice day, watching where she put her feet when she was climbing, cautioning Danny to do the same.

It took them about thirty minutes to reach their destination. Bessie got there first. She rounded a little hill and caught her breath. There it was. Her waterfall. It was more lovely than ever. She was still standing there, just looking, when Danny hopped over a rock.

"BOO!" he yelled, which startled Bessie so that she dropped the lunch. That threw him into fits of laughter whereupon she grabbed a tin cup, dipped it into the cold stream and threw the water on him.

"Now, no more," she giggled as he started to reciprocate. "I'm starved."

They chose a grassy spot away from the falls where the spray from the water couldn't reach them but which was close enough to the water that they could stretch out full length and touch it.

"I hope you like egg sandwiches, Danny."

"I never complain about what I eat. Sounds good. Look. To your left."

A Stellar Bluejay had landed in a pine tree, and was squawking at them so loudly that they were sure every wild creature around knew that intruders had come.

Bessie looked up at him and said, "Just never mind. We have a right to be here, too. And we're not leaving until we are good and ready. Here!" She threw him some little bits of bread.

He hopped down lower, still squawking, his black topknot bobbing about as he cocked his head to one side and then the other. He looked first at her and then the bread. Then he swooped in, grabbed a piece and flew into a tree to eat it, his royal blue coat rivaling the sky for beauty.

After she tired of feeding him and was full herself, she jumped up, ran to the rocky hill and began to climb to the top where the waterfall tumbled over the bluff.

"Come on, Danny," she shouted. "Let's see what's up here!"

"Go ahead," he yelled back. "I'll be up pretty soon. I want to explore that ridge over there," he added, pointing to a cropping of rock that seemed fairly bare of trees. "Maybe I'll find a cave or something."

"See you later then," she said and continued to climb until she had made her way over the last few feet of the hill.

"Ohhhh," she breathed. "How beautiful!" There was forest everywhere except for a flat, green strip of clearing, like a little valley, stretching back and away from her. The tiny stream, that turned into the waterfall, ran through it like a little shining path that led to adventure. She walked to the edge of the trees, hiked parallel to the clearing for a distance and then sat down to wait. It was an ideal place for deer. Perhaps, if she were quiet...

She was soon rewarded. Across the clearing, a buck sauntered out, his antlers magestically bobbing back and forth. With him were a doe and two spotted fawn.

They walked down to the little stream, the doe stumbling a little. Bessie shaded her eyes and watched her carefully. There was only one doe that she'd ever seen who stumbled. Could it be Tripsy? She strained her eyes, holding her breath as they drank and then moved downstream.

As they drew closer, she grinned. It was Tripsy, all right! There was the light tan cross on her neck. And those were the twins she had seen.

"So that's your husband, Tripsy," she whispered, her eyes sparkling. "He's a handsome guy."

The little family was wandering slowly around, munching grass contentedly, and she was debating whether or not she should let them know she was there. If she did, the buck and fawn would be frightened, of course, but Tripsy would know who she was.

Just then she was distracted by a bright flash at the forest edge across the small meadow. The deer family blocked her vision, so she stood up very slowly and quietly, trying not to spook them, and stretched her neck.

She gasped, "A HUNTER! It's a HUNTER!!" He was on one knee, his gun trained on Tripsy and her family!

Just then a CLICK echoed against the valley wall. The deer, alerted, swung their heads up, looking in the direction of the noise.

If Bessie had stopped to think, she wouldn't have done what she did next. But in her concern for Tripsy and her family, she began to run down the embankment and across the opening, straight toward the deer and the hunter, waving her arms wildly.

"DON'T SHOOT!" she screamed. "DON'T SHOOT! TRIPSY, RUN! RUN! RUN!"

Several things happened all at once then. Danny, who had entered the valley just in time to see what was happening, started toward Bessie on a dead run, intent only on the danger she was in. As for Bessie, she saw a blur of tan as the deer leaped into the air, and a sharp CRACK cut the quietness. Suddenly she fell to her knees, as if she had been knocked down, her arm burning like fire.

Grabbing it with her hand, she stumbled to her feet and went on, running and screaming, "STOP! QUIT SHOOTING!"

She caught a glimpse of a surprised and shocked hunter as she changed her course and stumbled into the forest where Tripsy had gone.

She was still yelling for the deer to run, when she tripped over a log and fell full length, and as she fell, she hit her head on a tree root which flooded her mind with a myriad of interesting sensations. Vaguely she thought of the Fourth of July and the fireworks she had seen once.

She rolled over on her back, groaning from the pain in her head, and then lifted her hand to shut out the sun. Her eyes widened and she stared hard. She couldn't believe what she saw! She moved her hand closer.

"Blood?" she whispered. It was dripping from her fingers. "How did I get blood on me?" She tried to think it through, but her thoughts wouldn't work just right. Then she remembered. "The hunter. He must have gotten Tripsy, and when I touched her..."

She continued to stare at her hand. She hadn't touched Tripsy! Tripsy must have fallen somewhere, shot, or she was gone, running as fast as the wind up the mountain, trying to protect her babies.

If she hadn't touched Tripsy, then why...and suddenly she understood. She reached for her arm. Yes, it was all wet. She drew her hand back and looked at it again. The blood was hers! She had been SHOT!

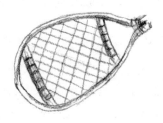

Chapter 18
The Angel

"I've got to get help," Bessie told herself but when she tried to rise, a dizziness overwhelmed her and she sank back onto the pine needles.

It was then she felt a soft touch on her cheek. She turned her head and then blinked her eyes, unbelievingly.

"Go away, Tripsy," she tried to yell, but her voice was barely above a whisper. "Please go away. He'll kill you."

Instead, the deer pressed her nose on Bessie's face and pushed against her.

Bessie reached up and scratched her friend's ears. "It's all right, Tripsy," she said with difficulty. "If I die, I'll just go to heaven. Don't feel bad. It wasn't your fault."

But then she wondered. Would she really go to heaven? She thought again of the door the preacher had talked about, the door that one was supposed to go through to get out of the devil's prison. Jesus had something to do with it, but she still couldn't figure out just what.

Her arm was hurting terribly. She tried to get up again, but the blackness came momentarily and she fell back down.

Tripsy nuzzled her hair. She put her hand on her pet's neck. Would Tripsy get to go to heaven, she wondered? Some animals were just naturally mean but Tripsy was so good.

She could hold her eyes open no longer. She felt Tripsy tremble under her hand. Then she thought she heard some brush crackle. Maybe the angels were coming through the forest to get her. Or was it the devil?

She heard a man's voice, but it was very faint. It was then she decided she must not have gone through the door to Jesus, because the voice cursed and said, "Would you look at that!" The angels wouldn't curse, she knew, so it must be the devil who had come. Bessie began to cry.

After a bit, she forced herself to open her eyes one more time. This time she saw a man. If he were the devil, the devil was someone she had seen before, but who? He was holding a gun.

"Run, Tripsy. He'll kill you," she tried to say again, but nothing came out, and she remembered no more after that, except it seemed she was dreaming, many parts of dreams that piled up on top of one another so none of them made any sense.

In her dreams, she saw Tripsy racing through the forest with a bullet chasing her. But Tripsy turned into the hunter with tears in his eyes, lifting Bessie up in his arms. Danny was there, too, saying something to her, but she couldn't hear him. Then the Stellar Jay swooped into the picture, swimming in the stream, and grabbing her sandwich.

Once she felt something cool on her forehead, like a soft breeze on a summer's day, and she thought she saw her mother's worried face staring down at her. Another time she saw Leslie in her dream, plain as daylight! She was there. And she was looking at Bessie, her eyes full of fear.

Things like that.

Then the dreams seemed to be less confusing and she heard a man's voice say, "We don't dare move her. She's lost too much blood. Go to Groveland as fast as you can, Johnny. If the doc's in, get him up here. Meanwhile, Mrs. Quimby, we will do all we can. The rest is up to the good Lord."

She knew then that she wasn't dead yet, and the devil hadn't come to get her, because that was Mr. Crocker's voice. That was for sure. But she wondered if maybe she was crazy, because she felt someone take her hand ever so gently and say, "My Daddy didn't mean to shoot you, Bessie. Please don't die. I won't be mean to you anymore if you'll just live."

"Whose daddy didn't mean to shoot me?" she wondered, as the sounds faded and she went -- who knows where? Wherever it was, as Bessie hovered between death and life, she saw an angel. She knew it was an angel because he was all in white and had big wings. He was looking at her solemnly, almost as if he were waiting.

She whispered to him, "I can't go just now, all right? My mother and father need me. They were real sad when my sister and brothers died."

But he didn't say anything. He didn't smile, either. So she tried again.

"Please let me stay. I'm not real sure I've gone through the door to Jesus yet. And I want to."

That was when the angel faded away.

After that, in her dreams, she saw the little stream in the valley above the waterfall again. But instead of the deer family, there

were sheep there, and she was one of them, lying in the grass, feeling totally safe, because a kind Shepherd was there watching over her.

One day, she heard familiar sounds. The clock was ticking. Coffee mugs were clinking. Wood was crackling in the cooking stove.

She opened her eyes. Looking down at her was her father. And then her mother's face appeared. She looked at them carefully. Her father was so handsome! And her mother beautiful. She hadn't remembered that.

"Princess?" her father said quietly.

"Hi, Daddy. Did you find the gold?"

That's when her mother burst into tears. Bessie stared at her, amazed. She had never seen her cry. Tears were sliding down her father's face, too.

They stepped aside for a chunky, kind looking man who checked her pulse and listened to her chest through a stethoscope.

"You must be a doctor," she smiled, but before he could reply, another face appeared then, and she gasped! It was the hunter! She knew now why he had looked familiar. It was Mr. Blackman, Leslie's father. Quickly he stepped back out of her sight.

"No, don't go away," she said, trying to sit up. But the doctor made her lie down again.

"You can't get up yet, young lady. You've got some mending to do now that you are out of danger."

"Did he kill Tripsy?" she asked. "Did he?" Then the hunter's face appeared again.

"No, Bessie. I didn't kill her. I didn't know she was your pet. I didn't know. I'm sorry I shot you," and Bessie was astonished again, because, except for her father's tears a few moments before, she had never seen a man cry, actually cry, but that was what he was doing now.

"Tripsy is just fine, Bessie," she heard her father say.

"And you'll be fine, too, young lady," the doctor added. "Your mother has something for you to drink, and then I want you to get some rest. You must get your strength back."

After the bitter sweet drink, she was so tired, she was glad to lay back and go to sleep again. The angel had let her come back and Tripsy was all right. That's all she needed to know right now.

Bessie was sitting up and eating a little bit two days later. But she still felt weak, her head hurt and her arm was really sore. So she wasn't allowed out of bed.

"How long have I been here?" she asked her mother, who put down a magazine she was reading and looked at her, smiling.

"Ten days."

"Ten! Did I really get shot, Mother? Or was I sick just because I hit my head?"

"You really were shot," she said, a shadow crossing her eyes. Then she smiled, "The bullet went right through your big fat upper arm."

Since Bessie had a very skinny upper arm, they both laughed. But it hurt to do that, so her mother didn't try to be funny anymore.

"Thank God, it didn't hit a bone. It'll take a while to heal, but it will be normal."

"I...I don't remember everything that happened."

"Well, actually, the hunter was aiming at the buck Tripsy was with. But they all got away."

"Tripsy came back to me, Mother. She didn't run." And then she frowned. "Unless I was just dreaming that."

"No, you weren't dreaming that. When Mr. Blackman finally found you, he saw her standing over you, pushing your face with her nose and saw you scratching her ears. He also heard you say, 'Run, Tripsy. He'll kill you.' "

"Did she run?"

"No, she didn't. Tripsy looked up at him as he stood there, and he swears she was begging him to help you. She kind of pushed you toward him with her head."

"Tripsy did that?"

"Can you imagine? Then she walked back into the forest and watched him. She was trembling when he walked over to you, but she stood her ground, and when he picked you up, she followed him, at a distance, all the way down the mountain."

Bessie just stared at her mother, trying to picture that.

"She risked her life...for ME!" she said, her voice reflecting the wonder of it.

"Yes. Well, you risked your life for her. Somehow, I think she understood that."

"Did she come to the cabin?"

"Almost, but not quite. She was out there for an hour or more, and then I called to her. I told her we'd take good care of you. I don't know if she understood or not, but she moved her head up and down, up and down, and then she turned and bounded off. She has come back every day since."

"So the hunter was Mr. Blackman. Did I see Leslie while I was sick?"

"Oh, she came up here several times before they left. It's the first time I've seen her act like a nice little girl.

"And guess what Mr. Blackman said?"

"I don't really care. I don't like him much."

"He said he was never going deer hunting again."

"He said that?"

"Yes. He was really upset that he not only almost killed you, but that he almost killed your special little friend. Then he worried about how he might have killed her family.

"He wept like a child, in front of everyone, even more than he did when you saw him. And he refused to leave our house all that first night. He just sat in a chair and stared at you, shaking his head. Finally I got him to go lay down and sleep awhile, but he only stayed in there an hour. Then back he came to sit by your side."

"What about Danny?"

"Danny was running across the meadow to try to help you but before he could get close, the bullet hit you and then you got up and ran into the woods. He searched for you until after dark, calling and calling, long after Mr. Blackman brought you down the mountain. He came stumbling in to the cabin, frightened half to death. Was he relieved to see you lying there, but when he saw you were unconscious, he went white as a sheet.

"Oh, and guess who else came several times to ask about you? Your friend, Bright Star."

"Bright Star came?"

"Yes, and she brought herbs and Indian medicine. The doctor let her put one of her poultices on your arm."

"Did it work?"

"Yes, he said it was excellent. It hastened the healing."

"Who went for the doctor?"

"Johnny Crocker. He's been in to see you several times, too. Your father came home four days after it happened."

She fluffed the goosedown pillows, and then looked at her daughter, clucking her tongue.

"I can't understand why in the world you did such a foolish thing," she said.

"I can't understand it either," Bessie answered.

They looked at each other solemnly and then Theodora smiled with a special twinkle in her eye. That started them laughing again, and even though the jiggling hurt Bessie's arm, and started it bleeding a little, she kept right on, until her sides ached.

Chapter 19

The Mountain's Secret

As May strutted its arrival with the brilliance of roses and basked in patches of wild iris, Bessie was beginning to feel like herself again, although of necessity, she was instructed to keep her arm in a sling until it was totally healed. She had not, for a moment, forgotten the pressing need they had to find gold and avoid the dreaded move to San Francisco.

"We shouldn't stop looking, Daddy," she said.

But in his heart, because he had tried for so many years, Thomas was convinced now that he would never find enough gold to support them adequately. However, since hope runs high in a child's heart, and not wishing to discourage her until it was absolutely necessary, he hedged.

"No, Princess. You aren't strong enough yet."

But his daughter was wise beyond her years and sensitive to the feelings of others. She looked at him for a moment, hesitating. Then she urged, "Please don't give up, Daddy. It's there. I just know it is."

And somehow her confidence struck a chord with his, and he

thought there might be a possibility after all. "You're right, Bessie girl," he stated positively. "We're going to find that gold!"

But one day about two o'clock, he came into the woodshed, hung his miner's instruments on the wall and entered the kitchen. Calling to Bessie, who was outside, he settled in his favorite chair and waved his hand for her to come closer. She wanted to climb up on his lap to comfort him, as she used to when she was small, for he looked so defeated, but he set a little stool right in front of his chair and asked her to sit there. Theodora leaned back in her rocker. No one said a word at first. All that could be heard was the ticking of the clock.

"Uh-uh-uh-uh-uhmmm," he began, clearing his throat. "I hate to say what I'm going to, but things aren't working out for us up here like I'd hoped. I'm going to have to take a job in San Francisco."

Bessie wanted to cry and beg him not to do it. But she just looked down at her hands and kept still.

"See, here's the letter I got, asking me to come to work." He handed it to Theodora, a letter that had been folded and unfolded many times. "The job isn't available until July, so I'll keep doing what I can around these parts. And, Princess, I'll continue to search for the source of your gold dust. But I'm afraid..." He looked so forlorn that she jumped up, put her arms around his neck and kissed him on the cheek.

"It's okay, Daddy." And then she went into her room and lay on her bed, staring at the ceiling. In her hand was the letter which offered her father the job. She had picked it up as she left the room. Maybe...maybe if she showed it to God, and prayed real hard, He would help them in some way.

She kept the letter in her pocket wherever she went, so she could touch it, every now and then, and remind God about it.

Thomas earned as much money as he could, going from one place to another, and on off days, he would pan upstream. Bessie's arm was still not healed, so there was little she could do, but she made valiant efforts to pan with one arm.

In early June, despite a certain nippiness in the air, two weeks of steady sun melted the last of the mountain snows, and the runoff water flowed quite vigorously.

On one flower scented morning, Thomas left for Crocker's,

Theodora dove into her darning, and Bessie stepped outside the cabin. She had slipped on her coat, which she left hanging open as always, for, despite her recent accident, she was a healthy and free spirited young lady, who chafed at buttons, hooks and caps.

"Whoaaa," she said, coming to a stop. "Look who's here! Hi, Tripsy! Where's your children?"

The graceful animal was standing only a few feet from the cabin, close to the runoff, reaching for some branches on a tree. The runoff water slid by their cabin and into a little gully that creased the slope down to Tioga road which curved to go northeast.

Bessie walked toward her friend.

"Here, Tripsy, I'll pull some fresh grass for you," she said. The doe took all she offered, perhaps remembering when she was a fawn and Bessie fed her by hand.

Bessie, whose arm was aching a little, tired of it before long, and had decided to get on with her panning when the sun flashed a message to her. Just beyond the deer, a sparkle of yellow came from the water.

"Move aside, Tripsy," she said softly, pushing gently on her rump, her heart beating rapidly.

She slipped her hand into the icy water. The object she had seen, about the size of a pullet egg, only it wasn't smooth or symmetrical, was lodged in between two rocks. She tugged at it, pulled it free and dropped it. It floated down to the bottom again, this time disappearing under a rock that was too far to reach from the bank.

She looked around to see if Theodora were watching her. Then she stripped off her shoes and stockings, pulled her skirt up, tucked it into her belt and stepped into the runoff. It was so cold, she lost her breath for a moment. She began to manuever her way out to the spot where she had last seen the object.

"BESSIE!" her mother yelled so loudly, and with such shock in her voice, that she lost her balance and sat down unceremoniously, the water swirling up to her waist.

Theodora was there in an instant, helping her out, scolding and shaking her and bustling her into the cabin.

"You'll catch pneumonia," she said, speaking rapidly, stripping her clothes off and rubbing her down with towels. "You aren't well enough to wade in snow water, you foolish child."

Pneumonia was no small threat, Bessie knew. They had known several people who had contracted it and died. So she didn't protest while she was wrapped up in a big quilt and set to drinking a cup of hot coffee which she drank, even though it nearly gagged her. Her mother then started a fire in the potbellied stove.

"Honestly, Bessie, about the time I think you're growing up, you pull a trick like that. Whatever possessed you to do such a foolish thing?"

"M...m...mother," she said, her teeth chattering. "I f...f...found something."

"I'm sure you did. Here."

She had heated a big rock on the stove, wrapped it up and put it at her feet. Then she rubbed her legs.

"But...M...M...Mother," she started again, and just at that moment, her father burst through the door.

He took one look and asked, "What happened to you, Princess?"

"Oh, this foolish daughter of yours went wading, barefoot, in the runoff," Theodora said. "Then she fell in. She hasn't a lick of sense."

"L...look, Daddy!" Bessie laughed, and held out her hand, opening it slowly. "I found a really big gold nugget."

Theodora stopped rubbing her legs and stretched her neck to see while Thomas reached out and took it.

His voice was very quiet and he spoke very slowly as he said, "Tell me exactly where you found this, Princess."

"About twenty feet below the cabin in the runoff. Daddy, we've been working the main stream up above. Maybe...maybe we should work around the hillsides close by!"

He walked to the shed, got some tools, and headed out the door. Bessie desperately wanted to go with him, but her mother wouldn't hear of it.

She made some hot cocoa for her daughter, which tasted "...an awful lot better than the coffee," Bessie allowed, and helped her dress into some warm clothes.

When Thomas came in that evening, he looked, first at Theodora, and then at his daughter. They watched him, not saying a word.

"I think we're on to something," he said, very softly.

Mother let out an "Ohhhh!" while Bessie squealed, but he held up his hand.

"I'm not absolutely certain, you understand. But I've been

checking the banks and rocks near us. I've found quite a lot of gold dust, and another nugget. I'll go at it again in the morning. Then in the afternoon, I'll head below to file a claim. In the meantime, it is essential that you both say nothing to anybody! The Crockers included. Not that they would try anything, but the word could get out to the wrong people in a hurry. If we have found gold, I want to be sure a thousand people won't come up here to camp in our yard to take it away from us!"

Bessie didn't sleep very well that night, she was so excited, but she wasn't the only one. The next morning, over breakfast, her father laughed as he said, "I must have looked out that door a dozen times in the night, half expecting to see some claim jumpers there. I'm afraid my imagination is getting the best of me. It sure is going to be disappointing if we run into a dead end and don't find that gold."

Bessie sobered. "Daddy, I saw those two men that tried to bother the old prospector on Priest's Grade that time when we were moving here."

"You whaaat?" Theodora asked.

"They were headed up...uh, that way," she said, pointing. "Course, that was last fall, but..."

"No need to worry, Bessie girl," her father assured her. "They were trying to steal horses from the Indians up near Hodgdons two months ago, and Old Chief Grizzly got some of his braves to jump them and bring them in to camp. Seems the Chief has a granddaughter that speaks English. She interpreted, making it clear to those two buzzards that the Indians would take action, as is their right, if they caught them stealing from them again. The crooks took off and no one has seen them since. Besides, we're not taking any chances. Now, Mother, is my gold miner going to be able to go out with me this morning?"

Bessie was given permission and she bounced out into the sun, full of energy, thinking about Bright Star and how she had played a role in getting rid of Old Long Nose and Spitter.

"I promised Mrs. Crocker I'd help her with some tatting," Theodora said, heading down the hill. "Don't worry, Thomas, I'll say nothing, not even to her."

Bessie knew enough to keep quiet as her father worked in the rocks and dirt, checking, testing and talking to himself. After a long while, though, she had an idea.

"Daddy," she whispered, "excuse me for talking, but what about looking closer to the cabin?"

He stood up then and stared at the mountain.

"Gold has to COME from somewhere, Bessie," he said patiently. "I figure there must be a vein. Maybe the tail end of it is nearby and the rest snakes up through that mountain." Then he smiled at her and said, "But you can look if you wish."

She started about halfway between the cabin and the runoff, holding the shovel with her good arm and balancing it with her bad one. She dug several shallow holes because the ground was hard, and then decided that, even though it was difficult, she would try to go deeper. She was down about two feet when her shovel hit a rock and off came the handle!

"Darn!" she growled, exasperated, and then looked over her shoulder quickly, feeling guilty. She sighed with relief, remembering that her mother wasn't home. If she had heard her, she would have been punished.

"That's a minced oath, Bessie," Theodora would say. "The word may not sound like you're cursing, but you might as well be because that's what's in your heart. Learn to be thankful in times of stress, rather than angry and you'll feel better. Neither will you have to worry about your language."

"Well, maybe so," Bessie thought, "but if we don't find gold, our whole lives will be ruined, and I can't be thankful for that!"

Then she remembered the angel and corrected herself. "I guess I could be thankful a little, if I tried," she muttered looking heavenward for a second. She reached into the hole for the broken shovel and pulled it out. In doing so, she saw something that made her gasp.

She squatted down, stretched her arm and picked it up. Scraping some dirt off it, she suddenly leaped to her feet and started running.

"Daddy! Daddy! Come quick. Hurry! I think it's here. It's got all kinds of gold in it, I think. Daddy!"

He came on the run, looked at the rock in her hand, raced to where she had dug the hole, fell on his knees and scooped dirt out with his hands. He inspected it closely.

Because the shovel was broken, he scurried to the shed, and came running with a big scoop, which he ordinarily used for snow, and enlarged the hole until it was big enough to stand in. The next big nugget came up on the scoop. Then there was another, and another. Hunks of yellow rock. Almost solid! They looked at each other, so overwhelmed, they couldn't even speak.

At last he said, "Princess, remember what I told you? About not telling anyone?"

"Yes sir," she said meekly.

"Do you think you can keep a secret so well that only God and the angels know it?"

"And Mother?"

"Oh, we never keep secrets from Mother."

"I won't tell anyone in the the whole world, Daddy. I promise."

"No hinting, either. Sometimes people can just tell by the gleam in your eye."

"I'll look dull and bored."

"Then they'll KNOW something's up. Just be normal. The fact is, Princess, we've found gold."

All of a sudden, Thomas was whirling Bessie around through the air, laughing and shouting and whooping, until she was giggling so hard, she couldn't get her breath.

"Let's tell Mother!" he yelled, and, taking her hand, went running around and around the outside of the cabin yelling, "Mother, come out, Beautiful One!"

"Daddy!" Bessie laughed. "Mother isn't here!"

"You're right!" he yelped. Then, pulling her as fast as her feet would allow, he ran down to Tioga Road and headed downhill to go to Crocker's.

"Wait, Daddy! If we run around like this, everyone will know! "

"Right again!" He whirled around and headed up Tioga Road, instead of down, shouting and laughing.

They rounded a bend in the road, and Thomas pulled to a quick stop, sobering. Two men were walking down the hill toward them.

Bessie's scalp prickled. It was none other than Jack Gaston and Maxie, old Long Nose and Spitter themselves!

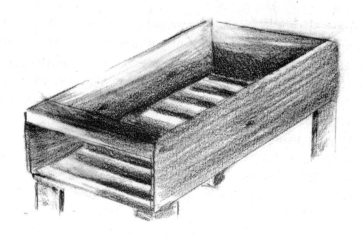

Chapter 20
Danger!

The two outlaws were not more than thirty feet in front of them, their guns raised and pointed right at Thomas.

"We've met befer, Mr. Quimby, if you'll recall." Long Nose said. "I tol' ya, I never fergit a face." They came closer.

"That was quite a while ago," Thomas replied. "I'm willing to let bygones be bygones."

"Not me," Long Nose snapped. "Unless you make it worth my while. We could hear yuh yellin' and seen you jumpin' and stompin' through the trees. Peers to me you found somethin' inturstin up yonder, right?"

Bessie had never seen a time before when her father couldn't think of something to say. She also never saw the time when she would speak up in the middle of a conversation grownups were having, because it just wasn't allowed. But she knew their gold was going to be stolen if something wasn't done, so, forcing a smile, she spoke up.

"My Daddy has been offered a job in San Francisco in July. He got a letter from the ship man himself. Maybe, in a few months,

I'm going to get a new dress."

She reached into her pocket and pulled out the letter Thomas had gotten.

"See?" she held it out toward the men.

Her father, seizing the advantage, reached for the letter. "Well, now, Princess, these men don't want to hear us bragging about how the Lord has provided. Course, if you're of a mind..." he said, looking at them, and pulling the letter out of the envelope, he began to read it. The men started to cough and move their feet and finally, Jake butted in.

"That's very interesting. Congratulations. Thought you might of struck gold the way you was carryin' on."

"Getting a good paying job is as close as some men get to gold," Thomas replied. "One has to rejoice and give thanks to the Lord for whatever provision he makes, don't you agree? Now, if you'll put that gun down, we'll be on our way."

The man's eyes went rapidly back and forth between Thomas and Bessie.

"We was goin' to suggest strongly that you sell this propitty to us, Mr. Quimby. You been prospectin' it?"

"Yes. I kept hoping. But hope isn't always rewarded."

"W'al mebbe we'll jist take a look oursefs. Jist in case. I mean, you mighta missed sumthin'. Now, turn around, put yer hands up high and march!"

But just as he gave his command, Bessie saw a movement in the trees above the road, just beyond Long Nose and Spitter. Then there was another, below the road.

Long Nose narrowed his eyes. "I said, turn around, kid."

"There's no need to involve my daughter," Thomas said. "Let her go and I'll cooperate with you fully."

"Let 'er go so she kin sound a warning? Fergit it, Quimby. Turn around, girl."

"Princess," her father said quietly, putting his hands up and turning. "Do what he says."

But Bessie was staring beyond their captors. "D...daddy, I saw Indians!" She blinked her eyes rapidly.

"Thet's the oldest trick in the book, girl," Long Nose said angrily. "Fergit it. I ain't aginst shootin' a kid, so git them hands up!"

But suddenly a female voice rang out, high and clear, "JAKE GASTIN! DON'T MOVE OR YOU'RE DEAD!"

At that, Long Nose froze, his eyes wild, keeping his gun on Thomas and Bessie.

She gasped as two braves jumped down onto the road behind the outlaws, bows drawn, arrows pointed. A slender figure stepped out from the trees and between the braves.

"I ain't afraid!" Jake shouted to the girl behind him, "Back off, Bright Star, or this little friend of yours won't live to grow up!"

"You are surrounded by our braves. Drop your guns."

His eyes wild and frightened, Jake swung his head to the left. Two braves stood on the bank, bows drawn, their arrows pointed at him. Three more, with guns, moved up from the bank below.

Suddenly, Thomas kicked Jake's gun hard from underneath, causing it to discharge. As the shot echoed through the mountains, he leaped on the claim jumper, knocked him down and held him there. Two of the braves had moved in quickly on Spitter, their arrows pointed at his chest and back. He dropped his gun to the ground. One of the rescuers kicked it aside and Bessie picked it up.

Bright Star walked to Bessie, her dark eyes sparkling. Bessie grinned. She didn't know how the Indians happened to be there, or why, but she knew that what had happened would make the bond between Bright Star and herself even stronger.

Thomas, pulling Jake to his feet, turned him over to two of the braves. He smiled at Bright Star and said, "Thank you. I'll return this favor someday."

"There is no need to return favors between friends," she replied. "Bessie gave us life. We give her life. It is as it should be."

Thomas looked at Bright Star and Bessie, not understanding, but aware that the two girls had something very special and precious going between them.

"I'll take these men down to Crocker's," he said.

Bright Star spoke in her language to the men holding Jake and Maxie, and they started off down the hill, Thomas following.

She looked into Bessie's eyes for a long moment, and then turned. As before, when she came to a bend in the road, she lifted her arm in salute and Bessie returned it. The two friends were parted again, their cultures so different that, beyond a visit, neither would cross into the other's, but their hearts would forever be one. They both knew that.

Bessie kept Spitter's gun with her as she climbed alone to the cabin. Picking up the gold they had found, she carefully placed it in a bucket and hid it in the woodshed. Then she covered the hole they had dug with a wide, flat piece of board. She rolled an empty oil drum over to the spot and wrestled it into place on top of the board, covering it with an oilcloth from the kitchen, and perching a jar full of wild flowers on top of that. She stood back to look at her handiwork. Yes, it would pass. If a stranger happened by, he would think a girl had been playing there, and would never guess there was gold underneath.

"You keep an eye on this, okay?" she asked a squirrel, who was peeping at her from a nearby tree.

She stared up at the mountain. "You knew all along, didn't you? This was your very biggest secret and you were keeping it for us."

And then, tired from the excitement and exertion of the day, she crept into the cabin, flopped on her bed and napped.

By the time she awakened, dusk was falling, so she jumped up quickly, chose some large potatoes and peeled them. If she hurried, she could have a celebration dinner ready by the time her parents came home. "After all," she said, "we have a LOT to celebrate!"

Chapter 21
The Pocket Mine

Everything but the gravy was made by the time Thomas and Theodora walked in. For fun, Bessie had put one big gold nugget at each plate, which set her father to dancing her mother around. As they ate, at her mother's urging, Bessie told her version of the day's events.

"What did you do with Old Long Nose and Spitter, Daddy?" she asked, after she had finished.

Since neither of her parents had ever heard her nickname for the outlaws, they looked at her, surprised. Then they both laughed until the tears coursed down their cheeks, a welcome relief from the tensions that had gripped them all.

When at last he could speak, her father said, as he took a succulent bite of asparagus, "Those rascals were locked up in a cabin at Crocker's, with a guard posted on the outside, and wouldn't you know, they tricked the guard into coming in, saying one of them was sick and going to die. They jumped him and escaped."

Bessie sucked in her breath, frightening memories of the claim jumpers filling her mind.

"Because of that, I had to tell the Crockers the whole story. We need protection for you two while I go below with the gold samples to see how pure it is and stake our claim. While I'm there, I'll notify the sheriff. He'll have enough evidence this time to lock those crooks up."

"If he catches them," Theodora said wryly.

"Oh, the sheriff is angry. He's determined to do everything that is necessary to get them behind bars. In the meantime Johnny Crocker and Danny Fields will be coming up in the morning to stay with you. Henry will be up later. I'm going to leave my gun. If you need to, use it."

"I have one, remember?" Bessie laughed, and pointed to the corner. "It was Spitter's!"

"I'll have to take that one as evidence, I'm afraid," Thomas said.

Not only did the boys come the next morning, but so did Celia. Bessie knew that Johnny and Celia both were good shots, because she had seen them shoot the heads off of game birds on the fly, supplying the Crocker table with both pheasant and duck.

Johnny stationed himself within sight of the spot where they had found pay dirt, camouflaging himself with bushes. Danny burrowed in not far from him. Mr. Crocker came soon, but stayed on a knoll overlooking the road. Celia, Theodora and Bessie remained at the house, with Celia sitting outside the front door with a gun, and Theodora keeping an eye out the back of the woodshed. Bessie was expected to take drinks and food out to the protectors. At times, she would go out to keep Celia company, and at other times, the boys.

Mother cooked dinner for everyone, and at night, they all bedded down in the house.

When at last Thomas returned, he was waving his claim papers, a big grin written all over his face. Everyone gathered around him, anxious to hear.

"We've got ourselves some really high grade gold," he said, so excited he couldn't sit down to the dinner Theodora had prepared. Then he grinned at Mr. Crocker, who grinned back. "I filed a claim. Come on, Henry, let's draw out plans as to how I'm going to get the gold out of that pocket."

As the men discussed it, Bessie asked Danny, "What's a pocket, anyway?"

"That's when gold has washed down from the mountain through the years, piled up in one place and stayed there," he explained. "It's hard to tell how big they are, Bessie. You might have one that will give gold for years, or it could be small." Then he added shyly, "I hope it's big."

Henry Crocker offered some old lumber so Thomas could build an extension onto the cabin, right over where he and Bessie had dug.

"It will keep your mine private and protected. And, when the heavy snows come," he explained, "you can keep right on working it because you'll be sheltered."

The two claim jumpers were caught a few days later and hauled off to jail, which relieved everyone's mind a great deal. With the immediate danger taken care of, Thomas decided he could handle the rest of it himself.

"But you can't get that ore out by hand, Tom," Theodora exclaimed one day as they were looking at the hole he and Bessie had dug.

"I can get an old arrastra for not very much," he explained. "Most folks have started using more modern methods of crushing their rock, so this old fellow I know has one he wants to get rid of."

"Will we buy a mule for it?" Bessie asked.

She had read about that in her school lessons. Mules had been used for many years to work arrastras. Tied to bars, they walked around in a circle all day long. Inside the circle was a heavy rock, or a hammer and large amounts of gold bearing ore. As they walked, the bars would move the rock or hammer, which would crush the ore into gravel so gold could be released.

Johnny had added to her knowledge by telling her what he declared was a true story. "There was this mule, see, which went around so many times, he got dizzy and fell into the arrastra."

"Oh, poor thing!" she cried.

"No, Bessie, that isn't the point of the story. The point is, they got him out but he was covered with golddust, so they had to comb him for hours to get it all. He was a gold mule!"

But Bessie, whose heart was tender toward animals and disapproved of any abuse, didn't think it was very funny. No mule should be made to live his life walking in a little circle, in her opinion.

So she was relieved when her father assured her, "The arrastra we're getting is a little more modern than that, Princess," he smiled. "This one is run by machinery, not mules. Come on, I'll show you what I have in mind."

He led them uphill and over to the right where the main stream was. "See, if we divert the stream about...here...we can run it this direction. I can build a ditch right through there at an angle toward the house. Be about a hundred and fifty feet long. Flowing downhill it ought to have enough force to turn the waterwheel which we'll build next to the cabin. Can you guess why, Bessie?"

"Well," she said, speaking slowly, trying to figure it out. "The water would turn the waterwheel and...oh! The waterwheel will probably turn the arrastra!"

"You're on the right track. The waterwheel will turn a shaft which we'll run into the shed we're going to build over the gold mine at the end of the house. That will make the machinery inside the shed work. The machinery will work a big hammer that goes down in the big hole that Princess will dig."

Bessie giggled at his joke as he went on, "And that big hammer will crush the ore. I'll haul it up with buckets, we'll get our gold out and be RIIIICH!"

He shouted the last word so loudly that Theodora and Bessie whirled around to see if anyone was near, and then they laughed softly.

Every morning after that, Thomas woke up singing and going out to work before breakfast, sawing and hammering and finally clanking machinery together that he'd hauled up on a wagon.

Mr. Crocker and Johnny helped him build the waterwheel which rose up magestically, poised to do their bidding.

Henry sent his other workers up to help, from time to time, so the entire project was finished and working by the end of the summer.

"See, Bessie," Thomas told his daughter when she asked about a long narrow box he had built, "this is a sluice box and you can learn to work it. We can separate flecks of gold from the gravel that we shovel into it by running water over it. The water carries the gravel and dirt out at the bottom and dumps it. It works somewhat like your gold pan. Now, see these riffles?"

She touched one of the wooden slats which ran from one side of the box to the other.

"Those are designed to simulate a streambed. You see, the gold is heavy and will sink down to settle behind them. Then, every few days, we'll clean it out. We'll even use quicksilver so we won't lose the real fine gold."

"Oh, the silvery stuff," she nodded. "I tried to pick some up once. It's wobbles worse than jelly."

"That's true. But it's very effective when it's doing its job. We'll pour that into the water, too. It sinks down, like the gold, and when it does, it sort of grabs the gold particles. That forms amalgam, a corky looking substance."

"Danny was telling me about it one day," she nodded. "Once you get that, then it has to be melted down, so the gold can get out again."

"Correct! You know, young lady, you're going to make a good gold miner," he laughed, tweaking her nose.

By September, some of their dreams were beginning to come true. The pocket mine yielded very richly, even though Thomas did all the mining of it himself.

One night Bessie overheard her parents talking quietly about the money they were putting in the Wells Fargo bank down in San Francisco.

"We have a small fortune already, Theodora," her father said with awe in his voice.

Before long he came home with a surprise for his wife, an elegant silverplated serving set, which included a coffee server, a tea server, a creamer and a sugar bowl. Her greatest joy, though, was when he bought a piano for her at Sherman and Clay in San Francisco. It wasn't a grand piano, like at Crocker's, but it had a beautiful tone and the keys were easy to play.

Then, of course, Bessie became the proud owner of several new dresses which she enjoyed wearing when she served at Crocker's or when they went below to Priest's Hotel.

Naturally, they were all predominately blue, in one shade or another, for Theodora continued to be insistent about that, but Bessie didn't mind. Anything was better than what she had

before.

One of them, her favorite, had such a metamorphic effect on her that Danny, when he saw her wearing it for the first time, felt as if he had been punched in the stomach.

"Don't you like it?" Bessie asked him.

Almost to the point of panic, he said nothing. He was flustered because his face was turning red. He could hardly be blamed for his lack of chivalry, however, because the last thing on earth he had expected was for Bessie to turn into a girl, and an extremely pretty girl at that. Up until that moment, she had been his friend, a tomboy, a fun fellow. Now she was someone who was causing all sorts of uncomfortable feelings deep inside of him.

"Uh...ummmm...well...uh..." he managed, whereupon she pressed her lips together tightly, planted her hands on her hips and said firmly, "Danny Fields, if you don't say something besides 'Ummmm' about the first dress I've had in ever so long that doesn't have patches, I'm...I'm going to..."

"It's...it's beautiful," he puffed out, motivated by her firmness. "I just didn't expect...it's just that..." He shoved his shaking hand into his pocket and pulled out a pink and milky white quartz rock. "Here. I...uh, want you to have it."

"Thank you, Danny," she said, turning it over and over as she inspected it, attempting to look reverent, for she knew how much it meant to him, even though she'd seen hundreds like it.

"You...you're pretty special, Bessie, and..."

She touched his arm and giggled. "Come on, Silly, I want to show you a toad I found. He's got the best warts!"

One night, after her parents had retired, Bessie rolled off her bed, shut her door, lit the lamp and pulled a little box out from the orange crate bedstand. In it were her most special treasures, among which were her first gold nugget, some letters she'd gotten from her father when he was away, a hanky her mother had crocheted, the quartz rock from Danny and a beaded bracelet Bright Star had made for her. She fingered each item tenderly.

But the one she took out was the letter from San Francisco, which had offered her father a job some months before. She turned her lamp down, and as soon as the flame flickered to

nothingness, she climbed back into bed and lay there with the letter held tightly against her chest. She looked up into the darkness, her thoughts carrying her through the ceiling, beyond the roof of the cabin and up into the sky where, she supposed, God lived.

"Thank you," she whispered. "Thank you for showing us the mountain's biggest secret. And thank you that we didn't have to move. I hope I can do a big favor for You, someday."

One day soon after that, while she was out in the woods by herself, she heard the pop of a branch, and turning, saw Tripsy. She held out her hand and her old friend walked over to her.

"Remember when I was shot, Tripsy, and you risked your life to stay with me? You know, I think it was a good thing all that happened. For one thing, no one hunts up here anymore, since the word got around. And Leslie is acting almost nice every time I see her.

"And, Tripsy, we found the mountain's big secret. We have gold now. But best of all, you know what? I saw an angel when I was unconscious. I did. It was an angel, I'm sure of it. I think he was waiting to take me away.

"And, when I said I wanted to go through the door to Jesus, but wasn't sure I'd done it yet, because I had bad thoughts about Leslie, and sometimes did things I shouldn't, I think that's when I did go through that door, because the angel went away then and I lived. And I haven't felt scared about not going to heaven anymore. That was God's secret, which was ever so much better than what the mountain had for us.

"I think you're going to go to heaven, too, Tripsy. I really do. Then you won't ever have to be scared again, either. Oh, Tripsy, I love you so much. Thank you for being my friend."

Tripsy nuzzled her neck, turned and bounded off into the forest.